'You and I have things to discuss.'

'Don't be ridiculous.' As the words erupted from her mouth, Elodie felt shame scald her cheeks. She hated rudeness. But this man unnerved her.

'If you had answered my letters you might have been spared this meeting. Have you been ignoring me in the hope that I would simply go away?' Neil shook his head. 'That's not my style. When I want something I always get it...eventually.'

Dear Reader

In this year of European unity, July sees the launch in hardback (September paperback) of an intriguing new series—contemporary romances by your favourite Mills & Boon authors, but with a distinctly European flavour. Look out for the special cover of a love story every month set in one of the twelve EC countries, which will take you on a fascinating journey to see the sights, life and romance, Continental style.

Vive l'amour in 1992—who do *you* think is Europe's sexiest hero?

The Editor

Before becoming a full-time writer, **Dana James** had a variety of jobs including police cadet, library assistant, and medical records clerk. Married, with a grown-up family of a daughter and two sons, plus a gorgeous little granddaughter, Dana enjoys travelling but is always delighted to come home to Cornwall where she has lived for most of her life. For relaxing she enjoys reading, horse riding, cliff-top walks, and weekends away in an ancient but much loved caravan.

A TEMPTING SHORE

BY

DANA JAMES

M I L L S & B O O N L I M I T E D
ETON HOUSE   18-24 PARADISE ROAD
RICHMOND   SURREY   TW9 1SR

First published in Great Britain 1992
by Mills & Boon Limited

© Dana James 1992

Australian copyright 1992
Philippine copyright 1992
This edition 1992

ISBN 0 263 77653 0

Set in Times Roman 11 on 11½ pt.
01-9208-50057 C

Made and printed in Great Britain

CHAPTER ONE

WEARING nothing but the briefest of bikini bottoms, Elodie lifted the heavy braid hanging over one honey-gold shoulder and twisted it into a coil on top of her head, anchoring it with two strong grips.

Secure in the knowledge that she was totally alone, and revelling in the warm breeze whispering over her body, she kicked off her sandals and ran down the beach.

The only sounds were the crash and hiss of waves breaking on the hard, wet sand, and plaintive cries from gulls perched on the rocks. The peace and solitude were bliss after the morning's frantic activity.

Sell this place? Never. It was the only proper home she had ever known. She had told Steven yesterday, and meant every word. The only way Munroe Developments would get this property was over her dead body.

And the inheritance tax? The dilemma haunted her, as oppressive as the summer heat. With her savings all used up, and her trust fund untouchable, how was she to pay it? In a couple of weeks she wouldn't even have a job.

She plunged into the waves and headed seaward. The cool water rippled like velvet over her sweat-dewed skin. As she swam she deliberately blanked her mind and concentrated solely on pushing her body to its limits, hoping that in the punishing physical effort she would find respite from a problem to which she could see no solution and from which there seemed no escape.

Taking deep breaths, Elodie dived beneath the swell. With powerful kicks she drove through the translucent water, enjoying the weightlessness and freedom of moving in several dimensions at once.

She finally surfaced, gasping. She blinked water out of her stinging eyes and wiped her face with hands that trembled from exertion.

Her heartbeat hammered in her ears and her breathing rasped, ragged and throat-burning.

She turned on to her back, needing a few moments to recover before beginning the long swim back.

She would never leave the valley. With so much of Cornwall given over to tourism there were few totally unspoilt places left. But, thanks to her grandmother, this was one. And now it was hers. She would fight with everything she had to keep it as it had always been.

The trouble was, she had little money left. How could she possibly make it stretch far enough to do all that was necessary?

As Elodie struck out for the shore, the muscles in her legs fluttered and tightened in ominous warning. She had burned up more energy than she realised. Every stroke was an effort. Speed and style, usually a source of modest pride, were forgotten. All that mattered was reaching the shore. How much further? She didn't dare look. Anyway, how could she see anything when her head kept slipping beneath the waves?

Suddenly, pain like a red-hot knife plunged into her calf. Groaning in agony, Elodie rolled over, inhaled water, and splashed to the surface, choking and spluttering as she fought to breathe. Her nose was running and tears poured down her contorted face. From the back of her knee to her ankle the muscle felt as though it was being crushed in a vice.

Drawing her leg up, she clutched at her calf. Her eyes, nose and throat stung and burned as waves slapped into her face. She fought the urge to shout. With no one to hear her it was a dangerous waste of energy. She tried to remember her life-saving drill, but the pain was like a thick dark blanket, smothering her ability to think. Her strength was ebbing fast.

Suddenly a swift dark shadow passed beneath her. Then a muscular arm slid diagonally over her right shoulder, across her naked breasts, and caught her firmly under the left armpit.

A split second later her chin was held fast in the palm of a large strong hand, and beneath her shoulders she felt the hair-roughened warmth of a man's chest.

All this registered in the few moments of paralysing shock before her survival instinct took over and she screamed, choking on a mouthful of sea water.

Galvanised by terror, she lashed out with feet, fists and elbows. The pain in her calf was excruciating. Above the frenzied splashing and her own gasps she heard him shout as some of her blows connected, but she was too panic-stricken to make out the words.

Though her chin was freed, the arm around her body didn't relax. Instead it tightened, hard. She couldn't breathe.

Powerful legs with muscles like iron encircled her hips and slid down to close tight about her thighs. Imprisoned, unable to move, Elodie was plunged beneath the surface. At first even more frantic, her struggles weakened, becoming aimless as the desperate urge to breathe banished every other thought.

Her lungs were about to explode and there was a red mist in front of her eyes. She couldn't hold out any longer.

They shot to the surface. Never had air tasted so sweet. Elodie dragged it into her tortured lungs with great heaving gasps, then started to struggle again.

'Stop it. Be *still*, woman,' a deep male voice roared in her ear.

'Get away from me.' Elodie's voice was half-shriek, half-croak from the mingled effects of fright and the sea water she had swallowed.

'Keep still or I'll take you under again. I mean it,' he warned as she continued to wriggle and squirm in an effort to break free.

His legs tightened around her once more and, realising he had every intention of carrying out his threat, Elodie stopped fighting. He had almost drowned her once. The next time he might well succeed.

Knowing she was far stronger than her slender frame suggested, she had never doubted her ability to take care of herself. So the terrifying ease with which he had subdued her struggles was a bitter humiliation.

While she had been thrashing about he had shifted his grip and now held her clamped against his chest with one arm around her ribcage. His other hand, across the front of her shoulders, held both hers and prevented her from hitting him again.

His right palm half covered her left breast. Either he was unaware of the fact, or simply didn't care. But for Elodie the brutal intimacy was a frightening illustration of her helplessness.

The sea, so cool and refreshing to begin with, was now numbingly cold. Except for the white-hot throbbing in her calf she was chilled to the bone. She clenched her teeth to stop them chattering and to hold back whimpers of pain. She had no strength left to fight any more. She just wanted oblivion.

A stinging slap jerked her back to consciousness.

'Come on, we're nearly there. You should be able to touch bottom now. Put your feet down. You're quite safe. I won't let you go. Come on, stand up. *Up*.'

Distantly Elodie was aware of a strong arm encircling her waist, half carrying her. Was that really sand under her feet? She swayed and staggered drunkenly, her right leg useless, the muscles knotted and set.

'Walk. Make the muscles work. It's the only way to free them.'

She winced, blinking back tears. 'It hurts.'

'The sooner you loosen up, the sooner the hurt will stop,' came the brisk reply.

'Oh, shut up,' she cried, hiding her face against his shoulder as pain stabbed and gnawed at her calf. 'What do you know?'

'Stop being so lazy. Make an effort.'

Lazy? The barb went deep. 'How dare you?' she raged, glaring up at him.

Sea water dripped from his dark hair and ran in rivulets down the hard planes of his face. Narrowed against the bright sunshine, his eyes gleamed dangerously.

'You have no right to call me lazy,' Elodie hurled her indignation at him. 'You don't know anything about me.'

'That's more like it.' He sounded pleased. 'The madder you get, the better. A shot of adrenalin in your system to boost your heart-rate and speed up your circulation is just what you need.'

'What?' Elodie's frown mirrored her confusion. 'Why?'

'I can think of several reasons,' he answered drily, 'but in this particular instance the idea is to get rid of the cramp.'

Clinging to him, she put more weight on her right leg, testing it gingerly. It felt badly bruised and throbbed like an abscessed tooth.

They had reached the shallows. As Elodie limped slowly ashore, racked by spasms of shivering, all she could think about was letting the sun's heat soak into her bones.

'So tired,' she muttered. 'I can't——' Closing her eyes, she slid from his grasp and stretched out on the sand.

From far away she heard him drop to his knees beside her, felt him lift her leg, then his strong fingers began to knead and massage her knotted calf.

She whimpered and bit her lip. But after a few seconds the muscle began to relax. The knifing pain started to ebb away and with it the tension that had gripped her whole body. As her calf returned to its former suppleness, relief and gratitude overwhelmed her.

The combination of the sun's heat and his soothing hands sent a delicious languor sliding along her veins. Then she felt the first twinge of unease.

Where his hands touched, millions of nerve-ends explored the contact, sending back messages to her brain which were becoming deeply disquieting. Something inside her was stirring. It shouldn't be happening. Not now, not like this. Not with *him*, a total stranger.

He had no right to be here in the first place. He was an intruder on her property. And now his touch had gone beyond simple first aid, and was an invasion into her very personal private space.

She didn't open her eyes, terrified he might see in them the feelings she was fighting. But she couldn't simply lie here. What was she going to do?

He tapped her leg lightly. 'You're tensing up again. Come on.' He took her hand. 'On your feet. I think you'll find that's cured it.'

Hating him for making her feel all these strange things she didn't know how to cope with, and hating herself for responding, Elodie stood up.

'OK now?'

She nodded, giving him a quick suspicious glance. Ironic amusement hovered at the corners of his mouth.

She looked quickly away. Then her breath caught in her throat. In her agony she had forgotten she was semi-naked.

To her total dismay she felt her breasts tighten, the rosy nipples standing out proud and taut, not from cold this time, but in involuntary reaction to the sheer sexual magnetism of the man beside her. Her embarrassment was so great that she blushed right down to her toes.

'I—I—my clothes——' she gulped, pointing up the beach.

He did not release her hand, but neither did the pressure of his grip alter. In fact he betrayed not the slightest reaction.

Elodie tried desperately to convince herself that he hadn't noticed. Then, to her utter confusion, she began to feel obscurely angry.

She should have been grateful for his apparent indifference. Instead she felt insulted. His lack of interest implied she wasn't worth looking at. But did she really want the alternative? Every curve and hollow explored by those piercing eyes? She shivered and, keeping her head down, started up the beach.

All that remained of the crippling muscle spasm was a very faint soreness. 'I presume that crack about my being lazy was just a ploy to make me react?' she demanded, grateful and furious at the same time.

'Desperate situations require desperate measures.' His deep voice held a sardonic note. 'It was touch and go for a while out there. You aren't the easiest person to rescue. I was beginning to wonder if I would have to knock you out. Fortunately,' he went on, 'almost drowning calmed you down a bit and I was able to tow you in without *too* much further damage.' He raised the hand holding hers to reveal livid welts and scratches down the inside of his arm, some of them stippled with blood.

Elodie swallowed. He wanted an apology? 'Am I supposed to feel guilty about that?' she blazed at him. 'You had no business being here at all. This is a private beach.' Her voice shook with an anger that was directed partly at him, but partly at herself

A TEMPTING SHORE 13

and the treacherous reaction of her own body. How *could* a complete stranger have provoked those urgent melting sensations?

'You are mistaken. I have every right to be where I was.' The polite but firm contradiction startled Elodie, but before she could demand an explanation he enquired silkily, 'However, that aside, what do you suppose would have happened to you if I hadn't been here?'

Elodie bit her lip, unable to meet his eyes. They both knew it was very unlikely she would have survived. He had saved her life. She ought to be grateful. And she was, only...

They reached her skirt, top, and sandals, which were lying in a small untidy heap. It seemed aeons since she had dropped them there. Breaking away from him, Elodie bent and snatched up her blouse. But, clumsy in her embarrassment, she dropped it. Before she could move, he had picked it up and was holding it out for her to put her arms in.

As he helped her, his fingers brushed her spine and lingered fractionally on her shoulders.

Flinching, Elodie leaped away as if she had been stung. She whirled round to face him, clutching the blouse tightly across her breasts.

'Who *are* you, anyway?' she cried. 'And what——?' The words died in her throat as she looked at him properly for the first time.

Thick dark hair was plastered in spiky curls to a deep forehead. High cheekbones and an aquiline nose gave his features a chiselled appearance only slightly softened by the ironic smile lifting one corner of his wide mouth.

But it was his eyes that had reduced her to tongue-tied silence. Cornflower-blue, narrowed against the sun, they glittered with amusement and something more, a challenge she didn't understand.

Apprehension quivered in the pit of her stomach.

He took a step forward, his eyes holding hers. She was transfixed. Even when he brought his head slowly down she was incapable of moving.

'I didn't expect you, Elodie,' he murmured, and touched his lips to hers. The contact was as light as a moth's wing and she trembled.

What did he mean, he didn't expect her? It was *she* who had been shocked and frightened by his sudden arrival out of nowhere. This was *her* land, she was used to having it entirely to herself.

His mouth moved on hers, at first gentle, coaxing, but growing hungry, and more demanding.

Elodie made a soft, wordless sound. Helpless, hating herself, hating him, yet unable to resist, she felt herself respond. Then delayed reaction tingled along her nerves like an electric shock. *He had called her Elodie.*

Pushing him away, she stumbled backwards. His dark brows rose, mocking her wide-eyed stare. In spite of the alien warmth he had ignited deep in the centre of her body, a chill feathered over her skin. 'How do you know my name?'

He shrugged, the movement drawing her eyes to his tanned and heavily muscled shoulders. 'How could I not know who you are?' His gaze travelled slowly over her and she realised with a scalding flush of dismay that she was still wearing next to nothing.

'Th—that's no answer,' she stammered, quickly fastening the buttons on her blouse with unsteady fingers. She stepped into her crinkle-cotton skirt and hauled it up over her hips, stuffing her blouse into the elasticated waistband.

'You've lived in the village for most of your life,' he pointed out. 'At the moment you are working in the local pub where, as well as cooking, you often wait on late diners in the restaurant. You're hardly a recluse. I could have learned your name from any one of a dozen sources.'

What he said was true and perfectly reasonable. Yet Elodie had a strong suspicion that there was far more to it than that.

Putting on her clothes had done more for her than simply cover her nakedness. It had restored a distance between them. She felt stronger and far less vulnerable.

Clad only in a pair of blue and white striped boxer shorts, he was the one at a disadvantage now. The trouble was, he didn't seem to see it that way.

With muscular arms folded across a broad chest dusted with dark, curling hair, his powerful legs planted firmly on the fine sand, he looked perfectly relaxed. But she'd soon change that.

'Thank you for helping me.' She tilted her chin, defying him to argue. 'I'd like you to leave now.'

He smiled and shook his head. 'Not yet.'

Elodie stiffened. 'You are trespassing. Didn't you see the notices?'

'Yes, I saw them.'

Elodie's temper began to rise. 'Then what——?'

'You and I have things to discuss,' he interrupted smoothly.

'Don't be ridiculous.' Even as the words erupted from her lips Elodie felt shame scald her cheeks. This wasn't like her at all. She hated rudeness. But this man unnerved her. Just the memory of being held close against his lean, hard body re-ignited the shimmering sensation that flooded her body with

warmth. She didn't want that. There were too many
pressures on her already. She had neither the time
nor the emotional stamina to deal with the inevitable complications that a man would bring to her
life. Especially *this* man.

He was a total stranger, yet some sixth sense told
her there was far more to him than mere good looks.
The intelligence and that challenging, knowing look
in those glittering blue eyes reminded her of something she had read about icebergs: the bit you saw
was only one tenth of their true size.

'I'm sorry, that wasn't very polite of me.' Elodie
picked up her sandals. 'But then nor is trespass or
assault.'

He gave a snort of amazed laughter. 'Dammit,
woman, I saved your life!'

'You threatened to drown me,' Elodie flared.
'And you almost succeeded. However——' drawing
herself up to her full five foot six inches, she made
a visible effort to overcome her anger '—your lack
of courtesy does not excuse mine.'

He inclined his head with mocking graciousness.
'I accept your apology.'

As Elodie battled to control her temper, the
suggestion of a smile hovered at one corner of his
mouth.

'If you had answered my letters you might have
been spared this meeting. Though, speaking for
myself, I would have regretted that. Have you been
ignoring me in the hope that I would simply go
away?' He shook his head. 'That's not my style,
Elodie. I don't give up. When I want something I
always get it . . . eventually.'

Bewilderment drew Elodie's brows together and her fingers tightened on her sandals. 'What letters? I don't know what you're talking about.'

'No?' He smiled and she had a sudden premonition of disaster. 'Then let me remind you. But first, allow me to introduce myself properly.' He made a wry face. 'In the circumstances formality seems rather out of place. But by all means let us observe the conventions.' He inclined his head in a semi-formal bow. 'Good afternoon, Miss Swann. My name is Munroe, Neil Munroe.'

CHAPTER TWO

FOR a moment the name didn't connect. Then an image flashed before Elodie's eyes—a distinctive logo on expensive stationery. Munroe Developments.

Feeling as though she had turned into very fine glass, that one more knock would shatter her into a thousand fragments, Elodie stared at him, her face a frozen mask.

'You could have saved yourself a journey, Mr Munroe. Unless your reason for coming down here was to get rid of me as well.'

His face hardened. 'Had I wanted to "get rid" of you, I have just denied myself the perfect opportunity.'

Recalling how he had forced her beneath the surface to stop her struggling, she shuddered convulsively. Only a few seconds longer, that was all it would have taken, and they would not be having this conversation. In fact, even holding her would not have been necessary. Once cramp had struck he could simply have watched and waited. The villagers would have shaken their heads and spoken sadly of 'the tragic accident'.

Elodie tilted her chin in defiance. 'We have nothing to talk about, Mr Munroe.' She turned away, wanting only to escape to the sanctuary of the cottage.

'I disagree,' he replied at once. 'You and I could talk for the next ten years and not run out of things to say. However——' he raised his voice slightly as she opened her mouth to deny his ridiculous claim '—I assume in this instance you are referring to the sale of the property——'

'*My* property, Mr Munroe,' Elodie flared. 'And it is *not* for sale.' If she had to work eighteen hours a day to raise the money to pay the tax, then that was what she would do. Provided she could find another job so near the end of the season.

'I understand your reluctance——' Neil Munroe began, but Elodie didn't allow him to finish.

'I doubt that,' she retorted, 'but in any case it doesn't matter. I'm not selling.'

For the umpteenth time she wondered why the tax couldn't be paid out of her trust fund. After all, the money was hers, or would be in two years' time. Meanwhile it was just sitting there doing nothing while her situation grew increasingly desperate.

He smiled his barracuda smile. 'We'll see.'

Elodie bit her lip as she watched him walk the few yards to where his own clothes lay strewn across the sand. It was clear from the area over which they were spread that the white T-shirt, faded denims and ancient trainers had been torn off and dropped in a hurry.

As he bent down he caught her eye. Her uncertainty must have been clearly visible for, raising one dark brow, he repeated softly, 'Desperate situations require desperate measures.'

Elodie's chin rose. Whatever had prompted his action, it certainly wasn't altruism. Neil Munroe's only interest lay in getting what he wanted. And what he wanted was this land. On no account could she afford to forget that.

'I was sorry to hear about your grandmother,' he said as he straightened up.

Elodie sucked in her breath. Though it was many weeks since she had found the old lady, in a small, crumpled heap amid her beloved daffodils, the sense of loss was still painfully acute.

'Why should you be sorry?' she said tightly. 'To you she was nothing more than a stubborn old woman standing in the way of your plans. A tiresome obstacle which, one way or another, had to be removed.'

Stepping into his jeans, he pulled them up over lean hips and fastened the zip. Encased in the well-washed denim he looked suddenly taller, broader, and more bronzed. He also looked angry. 'I find that remark offensive.' He bent to retrieve his T-shirt.

Elodie's fingers curled into her palms. Of all the self-righteous, hypocritical—— 'Do forgive me. Of course *you* aren't responsible. Your hands are clean. You employ other people to harass and bully and intimidate. You only concern yourself with results.'

Throwing the T-shirt down, he took a step forward and, grasping the nape of her neck with one hand, jerked her towards him.

'No,' Elodie said sharply. Stiff with resistance, she tried to back off. But he was too strong and once more she found herself unable to move.

His eyes glittered. 'You don't know anything about me.' He parodied the words she had so recently thrown at him.

'I know enough,' Elodie cried. 'I certainly don't want, or need to know more.'

'Oh, yes, you do,' he said softly, his gaze compelling.

She wanted to look away, but the force of his personality and the sheer impact of his physical presence made it impossible. She was trapped, held captive in the web of her own response to him.

Her throat was constricted, her legs felt weak, and her heartbeat thundered in her ears. She had to fight what was happening. She had to break his hold on her. Her tongue snaked out to moisten paper-dry lips. 'If it weren't for you, my grandmother would still be alive.'

His expression did not alter, nor did his grip slacken. 'For what it's worth, you have my deepest sympathy. But Hannah Swann was eighty years old and her health had been failing for some time.'

Elodie was racked by another shiver as she realised just how well briefed he was.

'To accuse me of being responsible for her death is both childish and unjust.'

Scarlet, unable to deny an element of truth in what he said, Elodie faced him. 'I don't see it that way, Mr Munroe. But then, I could hardly be expected to. I watched what your letters did to her as you piled on the pressure.' Disgust roughened her voice. 'Or are you going to tell me that they weren't your letters; that you delegated the task to one of your employees; that unfortunately he went just a little too far in his efforts to please you and secure the sale?'

Rubbing his thumb against the base of her skull, he drew her inexorably towards him. 'It really doesn't matter what I say, does it? Nothing is going to change your opinion of me.'

Instinctively her hands came up to fend him off. But as she touched his chest, instead of bunching into fists, her fingers slowly spread, threading through the dark curling hair, captivated by the warmth and texture of his skin. His heartbeat was a rhythmic, mesmerising throb beneath her fingertips.

His other arm slid around her waist and he began to stroke her back. He had no right. He was taking advantage of his superior strength. She ought to be hurling accusations at him. Why couldn't she get the words out?

The soothing repetitive movement was hypnotic. She could feel the warmth of his palm through her thin cotton top. Subtly the pressure increased so that with each sweep from her shoulder-blades to the small of her back she was moulded against him. The contact generated heat, demolishing the barriers offered by their clothes, and melting her bones. She could not tell where his body ended and hers began. Head spinning, heart racing, she surrendered to this new entrancing sensation like a flower opening its petals to the sun.

His grip on the nape of her neck relaxed and he cradled her head. Her breathing was quick and shallow and she hung helpless in his arms, subdued not by force but by an exquisite and intoxicating excitement.

Occasionally she had fantasised about meeting a tall, handsome stranger, about being swept off her feet by an instant and powerful attraction between them. But that had been nothing more than a romantic daydream, a momentary escape from the demands of a busy day.

Nothing in those dreams had prepared her for the disturbing reality of physical desire, the deep, yearning ache, the complete abandonment to abstracted sensuality.

Outside her experience it was beyond her control. Yet even though her own reactions appalled her she did not have the strength or the will to break free.

His hands slid up to cup her face and he studied her for a moment, his expression unreadable. 'In your eyes,' he murmured, 'I'm little more than a murderer.'

The vivid contrast between the feelings he had aroused and the impact of his words shocked Elodie out of her erotic stupor. But her swift intake of breath was abruptly cut off as his mouth covered hers in a kiss so gentle that her eyes filled with tears.

She didn't understand what was happening to her. What sort of person was she that she could allow it?

As he raised his head she kept her eyes closed and, with shame flaming her face, grasped his wrists and tried to pull away. But a tell-tale droplet slid from beneath her lashes, leaving a cool, damp track over her flushed cheek.

'Not quite so simple, is it, Elodie?' he said quietly.

She stiffened, opening her mouth to fling some retort at him. But as the tip of his tongue retraced the line of the teardrop her words died unspoken.

Releasing her, he picked up his T-shirt and pulled it on. 'I'll walk you home.'

'No,' Elodie blurted. 'I don't want you in my house.' She was afraid. Not of him, at least not directly. She knew he presented no threat to her in the usual sense. Instinct told her he would not demean himself by forcing his attentions on anyone unwilling to receive them. It was her own responses that terrified her.

'I hadn't expected to be invited in,' he announced calmly. 'Not this time anyway. We can sit outside. But, as I'm sure you realise, we do have to talk.'

Making an enormous effort, Elodie pulled herself together. 'Mr Munroe——'

'Please,' he interrupted, 'call me Neil.'

Elodie continued as though he hadn't spoken. 'I have a lot of faults, but I'm not totally stupid. You have no interest in me, only in my property. I have already told you, it is not for sale. If you thought that what has just happened would change my mind I'm afraid you vastly overrate your appeal.'

His brows climbed. 'You certainly don't pull your punches.'

'I'm sure your ego can take it,' Elodie retorted.

'And they call women the weaker sex,' he commented drily. The corners of his mouth lifted in a smile that raised the fine hairs on the back of her neck. 'However,' he went on, 'I find spirit tremendously attractive in a woman. I'm afraid I have little patience with feminine games.' The brief flare of cynicism that whitened his nostrils hinted that he was all too familiar with such behaviour. 'Honesty is far more... stimulating.'

Elodie was suddenly nervous. This wasn't the reaction she had expected. But then Neil Munroe was different from any man she had ever met. There was an intimacy between them which seemed to have bypassed all normal convention. An obvious explanation was the dramatic circumstances of their meeting. But knowing she could not afford to lower her guard when a small treacherous voice inside kept urging her to do just that was putting her under

enormous strain. Having to battle her own per-
fidious emotions gave her voice an edge.

'Don't waste your time, or mine, on compliments, Mr Munroe.'

'I wouldn't dream of it,' he replied smoothly. 'To
try flattering someone of your intelligence would
be a gross insult.'

Which was a flattery in itself. Recognising the
double-edged tribute for what it was, Elodie gritted
her teeth, trying to control her frustration. He was
far too clever. Even more dangerous was his be-
guiling treatment of her as an equal.

She couldn't help comparing it with Steven's patronising insistence on dotting every 'i' and crossing
every 't', except when he used legal jargon, which
he never seemed to find time to explain even when
she asked.

Appalled to find herself comparing this man,
whom she had known barely half an hour with
Steven, who had been friend as well as legal adviser
for three years, especially since Neil Munroe seemed
to be winning hands down, Elodie jammed her feet
into her sandals and glared at him.

'Elodie, whether or not it was I who dictated the
letters which caused your grandmother distress is
irrelevant. The company is mine. The buck stops
with me. I won't deny this parcel of land is important to my plans for the area. But your grandmother's death has not advanced my position in
any way at all. Instead of trying to deal with, to
use your own description, "a stubborn *old*
woman", I am now trying to deal with an even more
stubborn *young* one. In purely business terms that's
hardly a vast improvement.'

'What do you want, sympathy?' Elodie responded tartly.

Irony twisted his mouth. 'I get the distinct impression I'd be in for a rather long wait. No, I'll forgo sympathy in return for a cup of coffee and a look at these dragons I've heard so much about.'

Elodie's eyes widened. 'How——? Who——?'

'Bill Tremayne is a champion of yours,' Neil said lightly. 'In his opinion you are a very talented lady.'

What else had her boss told him? Just how much did Neil Munroe know about her financial position?

Ignoring the compliment she glanced up at him, her tone and expression both cool. 'What exactly is the point of all this, Mr Munroe? It should be clear by now that I have no intention of selling.'

He inclined his head. 'Indeed, you have made your feelings on the matter very plain.'

Elodie shrugged. 'Then I don't see that you have any choice but to let the matter drop.'

'You really mean that?' He seemed mildly surprised.

Elodie didn't bother to hide her impatience. 'What does it take to get through to you?'

'I have a suspicion,' he began slowly, 'that you may not be aware of all the facts.'

Foreboding slid like ice-water down Elodie's spine. Swallowing a sudden dryness in her throat, she tried unsuccessfully to ignore the apprehension clutching with clammy fingers at her stomach. 'And what *facts* are those?'

'My company has bought all the land on both sides of the valley from the road to the water-line. Which means I have you surrounded.'

Elodie swallowed again. She already knew this. But up to half an hour ago Neil Munroe had been no more than a name on a letter-head. Now the impact of the man himself and the effort it was costing to combat his effect on her gave those last four words far more significance than she would have wished.

'So?' was all she could manage.

Placing one hand lightly on her shoulders, he turned her to face the golden sand. She was acutely aware of him, of his musky scent and the warm weight of his arm.

'Show me the boundaries of your property,' he commanded.

Elodie eyed him suspiciously. 'You know perfectly well what they are.' She gestured. 'I own this side of the valley from the road down, and the whole of the beach.'

He nodded. 'In theory, yes.'

Elodie stiffened. 'What do you mean, *in theory*?'

'There is a two-foot-wide right of way which belongs to *my* land running down the south side of the beach. So you see I wasn't trespassing.'

Elodie turned a horrified face up to him. 'I don't believe you. My grandmother never said a word about any right of way. Nobody but us has ever used this beach. You're bluffing.'

Irritation clouded his features. 'Credit me with some intelligence, Elodie. Do you honestly think I would make a statement like that if I didn't have evidence to back it up?'

Hopelessness welled up in her. No, of course he wouldn't. He would realise she'd go straight to *her* solicitor and demand that a check be made. Elodie thought hard and fast. A right of way would have to be marked on the deeds. So Steven must have known about it. Then why hadn't *he* told her? Why

had he allowed her to find out from this man of
all people?

'Which means——'

'I know what it means,' she interrupted tightly,
and wrenched free, hugging her arms across her
body. It meant the loss of her precious privacy and
solitude, for, though no one else had used it, as
sure as birds flew Neil Munroe would, just to prove
a point.

'I don't think you do, entirely,' he warned. 'But
let's leave it for now. You've had more than enough
for one day. How about that cup of coffee?'

Elodie swung round, shaking her head in disbelief. 'You've got the cheek of the devil.'

He grinned, not in the least put out. 'I also have
the devil's own luck. It's not often I have the
pleasure of doing business with an attractive, intelligent, feisty young woman.'

'How many times do I have to say it?' Elodie
demanded, trying to ignore the appreciative gleam
in his narrow gaze. Now she understood the light
of challenge she had detected earlier. 'I am not
doing any business of any kind with you.'

'We'll see.'

'No, we won't,' she retorted promptly.

He smiled lazily and moved one shoulder in a
slight shrug, dismissing the subject as if it held no
further interest for him. Then, hooking his thumbs
in the pockets of his jeans, he glanced in the direction of the cottage, just visible through the trees.
'At least let me see the dragons. Please?'

Elodie hesitated. As he could be under no il-
lusion about her determination to hold on to her
property, there was no reason why she couldn't offer
him a simple cup of coffee.

On the other hand she certainly didn't want him thinking she was desperate for company. Nothing could be further from the truth. At the pub she was surrounded by people.

Apart from the customers, she had the wholesalers and the shopping to contend with. Then there was the kitchen help to organise. It was a relief to get away from them all and have time to herself.

No, the offer was just basic good manners, a token gesture of hospitality. After all, if he hadn't helped her she would certainly have drowned.

So, they would have coffee, then he'd be on his way. She would pass the whole matter over to Steven, and there would be no reason for her to see or speak to Neil Munroe ever again. In the meantime...

'It'll have to be instant, I'm afraid.'

'My favourite,' he smiled.

She shot him a look which was openly sceptical, and started up the beach.

'I mean it,' he said. 'It leaves more time for us to talk.'

The kitchen, which Elodie had always thought of as cosy, now felt claustrophobic. Neil Munroe filled it in a way no one else ever had. It wasn't that he was awkward or clumsy. Leaning against one of the work-tops, his arms folded, one foot crossed over the other, he appeared utterly relaxed as he looked about him with uninhibited interest.

His gaze fell on the dragon sitting among the potted plants in the deeply recessed window-sill.

Elodie watched out of the corner of her eye as he reached sideways to pick it up, his expression suddenly intent. 'Is *this* one of yours?'

She glanced up warily. 'Yes.' In fact it was her favourite. She had been experimenting with different glazes and this one had been a breakthrough. The basic colour was flame, but the tip of every hand-crafted scale and both tiny wings had emerged pearly silver. It was an effect she was trying to repeat, this time with a colour base of aquamarine and turquoise.

'It's beautiful.'

Elodie couldn't prevent a wry smile. 'You sound surprised.'

'Not by its beauty, or the workmanship.'

'Ah,' Elodie nodded. 'Just by the fact that *I* made it.'

'Not in the sense *you* mean,' he replied. 'You see, I already own one of these. I picked it up in London. I've been on the look-out for more, but none of the dealers and galleries I spoke to knew who made them.' He turned the dragon over, handling it with great care.

Switching on the kettle, Elodie set a tray. But no matter which cupboard she needed something from, or which drawer she had to open, she was forced to brush past him.

Though the three-foot-thick walls kept the kitchen comfortably cool even in the hottest weather, perspiration dewed her forehead as she cut slices of apple cake. Never in her life had she been so *aware* of a man.

'How long does it take to make one?'

Elodie shrugged. 'Several weeks. It's just a hobby, really.'

He shook his head. 'You shouldn't be wasting your time——'

Elodie flushed. 'Actually,' she interrupted defensively, 'I've managed to sell quite a few.'

'You didn't let me finish,' he chided. 'I was about to say you shouldn't be wasting your time doing anything else when you have a talent that can produce work like this. How much do you charge for them?'

The cups rattled slightly as Elodie set them down. 'Fifty pounds for that size and seventy-five for the larger one. I know it sounds a lot,' she added hurriedly, 'but it's mainly to cover the cost of materials.'

'My dear girl,' he frowned, 'these are a collector's item. They are worth at least five times that amount.'

Elodie gaped at him, stunned. His statement had quite literally taken her breath away. 'You're joking,' she managed at last, a disbelieving smile trembling on her lips.

'I never joke about money,' was his dry response. 'Would you allow me to take this with me? There's someone I want to show it to. Someone whose opinion I value.'

Totally bemused, Elodie made a vague gesture of acquiescence then switched off the kettle and poured boiling water into the cups. 'You will take care of it? Only——'

'I'll guard it with my life,' he promised.

'There's no need to be facetious.'

His gaze fixed on the dragon, he shook his head. 'You still don't understand, do you?' He looked up. 'Elodie, I'm serious. We have something very special here.'

Their eyes met and locked. It was a timeless moment. Then, in the depths of his, something stirred. What was it? Amusement? Sympathy?

She looked away quickly, and opened the fridge to take out the milk jug. He was referring to the dragon. Imagining anything else was not just ridiculous, it was pathetic. She was twenty-three years old, a grown woman, not some lovesick teenager with a head stuffed full of romantic nonsense. And this tall, handsome, immensely attractive man was Neil Munroe, a determined and ruthless businessman who wanted her land.

'Bill Tremayne was right.' Pulling several paper towels from the dispenser on the wall, he began wrapping the dragon with the sort of care she would have associated with a rare Ming vase. 'You are a lady of many talents.'

Elodie shrugged, determinedly ignoring the treacherous stab of pleasure at his compliment. 'I enjoy what I do.'

He said nothing, but the lift of his brows caused a tide of colour to sweep up her throat, burning her face as she remembered, just as he intended she should, the sensation of being pressed so close to him that the heat generated by their bodies seemed to fuse them into one being.

'It's much too nice to stay indoors,' she announced, avoiding his eyes. 'Let's go out on to the grass.'

He set the dragon down gently and she heard the undercurrent of amusement in his voice as he reached past her and picked up the tray. 'As you wish.'

Seating herself with the tray between them, Elodie pushed one cup and saucer towards him, withdrawing her hand quickly. She didn't want to risk his touch, accidental or otherwise. 'Please help yourself.' She gestured towards the thick, moist slices of apple cake with their crunchy golden topping.

Holding her own cup in both hands, Elodie sipped. The hot liquid curled like smoke in her stomach, making her realise how hungry she was. But tension would not allow her to eat, not while he was here.

'This is a very peaceful place,' he remarked, gazing thoughtfully around him.

'It always has been,' Elodie answered. 'That's what makes it so special. But it wouldn't stay like that for long if you got your way.'

'Change is a vital part of life, Elodie. Nothing remains the same forever. Without progress things simply stagnate and decay.'

'Progress?' Elodie snorted. 'Is that what you call it? Have you seen the new estate on the outskirts of the village? They tore up good farmland to build that...that eyesore. I'll lay you any odds you like that the architect who designed those houses won't be living in one of them. Calling them detached must be a contravention of the Trade Descriptions Act. Anybody sneezing in one would give a cold to the people next door.'

'But surely,' Neil countered smoothly, 'the important thing is that they are providing a home for someone who otherwise would not have one.'

'Rubbish,' Elodie scoffed. 'What first-time buyers could afford those prices? Almost all those properties have gone to people who have come down here to retire. I have nothing against that in principle, but it's getting out of hand. Local people are being priced out of the area.'

Leaning on one elbow, he studied her. 'What if I told you my plans for developing this land include houses for first-time buyers?'

Her look was scathing. 'You're joking, of course.'

His brows climbed. All right, maybe her response had been less than polite, but he had provoked it. Then she realised. He had done it deliberately. He had been sounding her out, testing her. Colouring, she opened her mouth, but got no chance to speak.

'No apologies, Elodie,' he warned. 'You meant every word.'

'I had no intention of apologising,' she retorted.

'Good, because as it happens you are correct. I specialise in luxury developments for the top end of the market. To remain in business I have to make a profit in order to invest in new projects. However, as I am considered good at what I do, I have never yet needed to resort to raping the land or hounding old ladies to an early grave.'

He swallowed the last of his cake. 'I can see you have no intention of accepting my word, at least not without proof. So I'd like to make a suggestion. By the way, that was delicious.' He grinned, reaching for another piece. 'I know one is supposed to wait until asked, but you might not offer, and I'm hungry.'

Elodie gestured helplessly. She was completely out of her depth and had a strong suspicion that not only was Neil Munroe fully aware of this, but that he had deliberately planned it.

He took a bite out of the new slice. 'Mmm, what spice is that?'

'Cinnamon,' she replied briefly. Then, replacing her cup with great care, Elodie moistened her lips. 'What suggestion?'

'I'd have thought it was obvious. You consider me a money-grubbing philistine; I believe I create homes which are in total harmony with their surroundings. We can't both be right. So I suggest I take you to see some of my completed developments.'

Elodie eyed him sceptically. 'Why should you care what I think of you?'

His gaze held hers. 'I can't imagine.' Dusting the crumbs from his fingers, he got smoothly to his feet. 'I'm afraid I have to go. I'll be in touch to arrange a date and time. May I go in and pick up the dragon?'

Scrambling to her feet, Elodie faced him. 'I haven't said I'll come.'

He smiled his barracuda smile. 'If you really care about all this——' his sweeping gesture encompassed the cottage and wooded hillside '—how can you afford not to?'

CHAPTER THREE

AFTER Neil Munroe had gone, Elodie washed up the cups and saucers, returned the rest of the cake to the tin, and went into the tiny lean-to bathroom to shower the salt water from her hair and, with it, she hoped fervently, the memory of his touch.

But as she tilted her head back, lifting her face to the needle-sharp spray, he was all she could see. Images of him were indelibly printed on the inside of her eyelids and no amount of will-power was strong enough to remove them.

An hour later, dressed in light cotton trousers and a baggy shirt, her hair spread like a bronze cape over her shoulders to dry, Elodie perched on the high wooden stool in her workroom, chewing slowly on a cheese and home-made tomato chutney sandwich as she gazed, unseeing, at the white clay figure of a half-completed dragon.

She felt . . . different. She *was* different. And it was Neil Munroe, barging into her life with all the subtlety of a dumper truck, who had caused the changes which she sensed, with a sinking heart, were irrevocable. His hands on her skin, the knowing glance which intimated a thousand shared secrets, and his amused, ironic smile had catapulted her into a new dimension of awareness.

As far as her dragons were concerned she had told him the truth. The pleasure she got out of making them was far more important to her than the money they fetched. Which was something

Steven had never understood. Not that his be-
littling attitude to her 'messing about with clay'
bothered her unduly. Other peoples' appreciation
of her efforts was a bonus, welcome but not sought.

Yet she had soaked up Neil Munroe's compliments as if they had been cool water in a desert.
Why? Why should she care what he thought? Who
was he anyway? A property developer, a modern
barbarian imposing his own will on the landscape
and laughing all the way to the bank.

But, try as she might to hang on to her indignation, it trickled away like fine sand through her
fingers as she relived the powerful and disturbing
sensations she had experienced in Neil Munroe's
arms, and that subtle, exquisitely gentle kiss. Aloof
and forbidding one moment, he could be lightly
self-mocking the next. He was manipulative, magnetic, and very, very dangerous.

Finishing her sandwich, Elodie tied back her
almost dry hair with a bright scarf and picked up
her shoulder-bag and a sweater. Sitting here fretting
wasn't going to achieve anything. It was time she
showed a little of the spirit he had so admired.

Stepping into the public phone box a few yards
from the Royal Oak's car park, Elodie glanced at
her watch then dialled Steven's office number. It
was only quarter-past five and he rarely left before
six.

Sounding harassed, the receptionist announced
curtly that she would see if Mr Lockwood was
available to take the call, making Elodie wince as
she clattered the receiver down on the desk.

Idly wondering what could have ruffled the normally placid Miss Collins, Elodie heard a door
open, then Steven's voice, clearly furious.

' . . . no excuse. You're a broker, for God's sake. It's your job to foresee when the market will fall. How much have I lost on the deal? *What*? Hold on. What is it, Margaret? I told you I didn't want to be disturbed.'

Elodie heard a brief and muffled exchange. A few moments later the receiver was picked up.

'Sorry to have kept you. Mr Lockwood is just coming.'

'Thank you.'

Brisk footsteps approached and the receiver was picked up again. 'Elodie? I hope this is important. I am rather busy.'

Clearly he hadn't had a very good day either. 'Then I'll be brief,' she replied. 'It's about this right of way down my beach.'

There was total silence for a moment. 'When did you learn about it?' he enquired.

'This afternoon. Steven, I do wish you had——'

'How did you come by the information?' he cut in.

'Neil Munroe told me. Steven——'

'Where was this? And why were you talking to him?'

His sudden hostility reinforced her instinctive reluctance to tell him in detail what had happened. She swallowed. 'He was trespassing on the beach and I tackled him about it.' Though a drastically edited version of the afternoon's events, it was the truth.

'You shouldn't have spoken to him at all,' Steven berated.

'In the circumstances I could hardly have ignored him,' Elodie retorted. Too late she wished she had held her tongue, terrified Steven would ask *what* circumstances. But he was too concerned with what he evidently saw as an undermining of his authority.

'All matters relating to the property should be handled solely by myself and Munroe's solicitors,' he insisted severely. 'That's the way these things are done, Elodie. I thought you understood that. If you talk to him yourself, heaven knows what sort of a mess we'll end up with. No offence, my dear, but you really must leave these matters to those properly qualified to deal with them.'

'Yes, Steven,' Elodie said, biting back the urge to point out that the very last thing she would have done was go looking for Neil Munroe. He had sought *her* out. But if she told Steven that it might lead to further cross-examination, the last thing she wanted right now.

'Neil Munroe is a cold, calculating businessman who puts profit above everything else,' Steven went on. 'Rumour has it that he's charming, but it's only a veneer. Behind the façade lie the scruples of a shark. I know people who have had dealings with him. They say he has as much human feeling as a machine.'

'Is he married?' Elodie was shocked to hear herself ask.

'How like a woman,' Steven sighed, and Elodie could visualise his condescending expression. 'The very idea is laughable. A man like him wouldn't waste time or energy on *marriage*. When it comes to women, he simply takes what he wants when he wants it, and moves on. No woman will tie Neil Munroe down.'

Elodie thought he sounded almost envious.

'He's a man with an eye to the main chance.' Steven's words were like hammer-blows. 'He's out for number one, and doesn't give a damn about anybody else.'

Elodie's heart thumped painfully and her grip on the receiver was so tight, her hand ached. His kiss had been an almost magical experience. Could it really have been part of a deliberate and cynical ploy? Was she playing right into his hands? Just another little fish being reeled in by an expert angler?

Doubts coiled like snakes in her mind, smothering her own evaluation of Neil Munroe as a hard man certainly, but one too self-assured to be anything but honest.

'You have something he wants,' Steven pounded on. 'You are also young and have no experience of dealing with a man like him. I am your only protection, Elodie. You must leave this to me. I'll handle everything. Look, I must go, my dear, I have a client waiting. But I'll see you soon.'

'No, Steven, wait——' she said quickly, but he had already cut the connection.

Elodie took the shallow tin from the oven and slammed the door shut. Marinaded in lime juice, Worcestershire sauce and rosemary, the chicken breasts had been roasted to golden perfection on a bed of chopped celery leaves and sautéed onion. Using a slotted spoon, she arranged the chicken on a bed of fluffy rice.

Would Neil Munroe eat here tonight? She hoped...what? That he would, or he wouldn't? Her mind was in turmoil. After listening to Steven she didn't know what to think or who to believe. But

Steven's warnings could not easily be ignored, especially as they echoed her own doubts.

Picking up the serving dish and the accompanying bowl of mixed salad, Elodie left the kitchen. It had been a hectic evening but these were the last customers. She should be on her way home within an hour. Though she had a feeling that tonight sleep would be a long time coming.

She pushed open the door into the dining-room with her shoulder. And stopped dead. Neil Munroe was sitting at one of the corner tables.

Only a few hours ago she had been nearly naked in his arms. She had watched him climb into faded jeans and a T-shirt, both of which fitted like a second skin, looking as though he rarely wore anything else. Yet here he was, darkly handsome in a crisp white shirt and maroon tie, the pale grey jacket of his suit hanging over the back of his chair.

Glancing up from the menu he was studying, he inclined his head. This rather distant courtesy was instantly negated by the lifting of one dark brow, a silent and intimate reminder of shared experiences.

With cheeks aflame, her heart thumping uncomfortably, and Steven's warnings ringing in her ears, Elodie ignored him and crossed to the couple who had ordered the chicken.

She served their meal, poured their wine, and made sure they had everything they wanted, operating on automatic pilot while her thoughts exploded in all directions like sparks from a firework.

Eventually she had no choice but to approach him. But, having decided what she was going to do, she was able to summon a diplomatic smile. 'I'm so sorry, I'm afraid the kitchen is closed for the night.'

Amusement lifted the corners of his mouth, and his mocking gaze brought goose-pimples up on her arms. 'I wondered if it might be, so I checked with the landlord before I came in. He assured me I wasn't too late.'

Elodie's fingers curled into her palms. His ability to be always one step ahead was not just uncanny, it was frightening. Steven was right, she was out of her depth.

'However, as the last thing I want is to keep you slaving over a hot stove, could I order a simple mushroom omelette?'

Gritting her teeth, Elodie gave a brief nod and turned to go.

'With a baked potato? And possibly a green salad?' he added.

Elodie turned back, her face carefully expressionless. 'Anything else?'

'No, that will be fine. As a matter of fact,' he remarked, his eyes gleaming like a cat's in the candlelight, 'I'm starving. Apart from some apple cake, I haven't eaten since breakfast, and physically it's been a very demanding day.'

The implication was unmistakable. As Elodie's colour rose so did her chin. 'Then I'd better get your meal before you're too weak to eat it,' she retorted, and marched out to the kitchen.

'That certainly looks appetising.' His gaze flickered over her as she set the plate in front of him. 'I've never seen such a fluffy omelette.'

Elodie's face burned. Her reply was brief and succinct. 'Practice.'

'Or temper,' he mused softly.

Elodie decided not to dignify that remark with an answer. In fact he was far too close to the truth. While preparing the food she had been torn. She didn't want to cook for him at all. Yet professional pride demanded she make the simple meal as appealing as possible. Worse still, seeing him again had rekindled all the emotions she had experienced during their time together that afternoon.

'Bill Tremayne's assessment of you as a lady of many talents was no exaggeration.' Shaking out his napkin, Neil laid it on his lap. 'You are living proof of the old saying that the way to a man's heart is through his stomach.'

Elodie gritted her teeth so hard, she wouldn't have been surprised to feel chips of enamel flying off.

'Mr Munroe, cooking is my job, and I enjoy it. But it is not the focal point of my life. Nor am I the least bit interested in using it as a way to any man's heart, least of all yours, though whether you possess one is open to question. And if, through some mental aberration, I *were* interested, the obvious route would be through your wallet, as *your* only passion is money.'

'Elodie?' Bill's voice right behind her made her start. She spun round. How long had he been there? It was obvious from his shocked expression that he had heard her blistering attack on Neil Munroe, and equally plain that he was extremely curious.

Elodie toyed with the napkin she had used to carry in the heated plate, frantically searching for an explanation which would satisfy Bill without provoking further questions.

Then Neil laid his hand on her arm, the fleeting pressure of his fingers a warning to her not to say anything, which was quite unnecessary as her brain seemed to have stopped functioning.

'There's no need to look so concerned, Bill.' Neil's tone held humour and reassurance. 'Nothing's wrong. Elodie and I have the kind of relationship which might best be described as...volatile.'

A variety of expressions flitted across the landlord's face as his glance darted from one to the other. After a few moments he nodded. Scepticism lurked at the corners of his mouth, but his tone was one of bemused acceptance. 'I didn't realise you knew one another that well.'

Her face on fire, Elodie kept her eyes lowered. What he really meant was, he hadn't realised they knew one another at all. Neil's easy laugh brought her head up in swift apprehension.

'Come on, Bill. You surely don't think someone as well-mannered and level-headed as Elodie would talk like that to a stranger?'

He made the proposition sound utterly ludicrous. But, knowing her behaviour had been the exact opposite, Elodie realised that Neil had chosen his words deliberately. He had rescued her from a difficult and embarrassing situation. But he would make her pay, of that she had no doubt.

'No,' Bill agreed, hesitant. Then, brushing aside any misgivings, he turned to Elodie. 'No, of course she wouldn't.' He shook his head, grinning widely. 'You're a dark horse, aren't you, girl? And there was me thinking you and that yuppie lawyer—which reminds me, he's in the bar. Says he wants to speak to you.'

Elodie opened her mouth but once again Neil spoke first. 'Could I ask you a favour, Bill? Would you tell the gentleman that Elodie is unavailable this evening?'

Bill winked. 'No problem. Can't say I'm keen on the bloke. I've always thought Elodie could do far better for herself.'

'My sentiments exactly,' Neil agreed, his bland expression totally at odds with the look in his eyes that rasped across Elodie's nerves, leaving them raw and quivering. 'By the way——' he turned back to the landlord '—I'm delighted to hear your wife is making a speedy recovery. Will she be home soon?'

The question was like a kick in the stomach to Elodie. Not only did it show how quickly Neil Munroe had acquainted himself with all the local news, it also revealed that he knew her job here at the pub was only temporary.

'Coming on fine, she is,' Bill beamed. 'I should have her back in a couple of weeks. Mind you, we'll miss Elodie. Been worth her weight in gold, she has. Well, I'd better go and pass on your message.' He left, rubbing his hands, clearly looking forward to the task.

Elodie tried desperately to pull herself together. 'Now just a minute,' she whispered fiercely, removing his hand with trembling fingers.

'Let me eat first, please?' Neil entreated. 'I can't handle all this emotion on an empty stomach. Go and do whatever you have to do, then I'll take you home and you can get it all out of your system. Someone has been dripping poison into your lovely little ears. I can guess who, but I'd like to know why.'

The imprint of his grip still lingered and unconsciously she rubbed her wrist, trying to erase the distracting sensation. Then she realised he was watching. Colour flooded her face. 'You are not taking me home,' she stated flatly.

The brief movement of Neil's broad shoulders beneath his hand-made shirt stirred treacherous memories of the warmth of his bronzed skin, and the play of muscle beneath her fingertips. Elodie swallowed convulsively.

Cutting into the omelette, Neil chewed on a mouthful. 'This is delicious.' He slanted a glance at her. 'You are not leaving here alone.' Though his tone was mild, Elodie glimpsed in his eyes an implacability that made her blood run cold. 'Make your choice, Elodie. It's either me or the yuppie.'

Furious, Elodie glared at him. 'Damn you,' she whispered fiercely and stormed out, oblivious to the startled glances of the other two customers.

Driven by a consuming anger, Elodie washed up and tidied the kitchen ready for the following morning. But her rage was directed as much against herself as at him. Why hadn't she simply told him to go to hell? She had indeed had more than enough for one day. She was going home by herself and no one, especially Neil Munroe, was going to stop her.

He had actually had the nerve to pretend sympathy though he had as much sensitivity as a juggernaut. Even worse, he had tried to convince her that they shared similar views and opinions.

Elodie scrubbed a roasting-tin with a sudden burst of furious energy as she fought the memory of her powerful and startling attraction to him.

Steven's warning and the memory of her grandmother's distress were too strong to be simply pushed aside.

What could she possibly have in common with Neil Munroe? They came from different worlds.

What did she actually know about him? All right, so he had awakened her body and stirred her heart, but could she trust her own judgement? How could her confused feelings about this man offer a sound enough basis for decisions which would affect the rest of her life?

After final coffees had been drunk, bills settled, and the other couple had gone on their way, Elodie began loading the remaining dishes on to a tray. She was acutely conscious of Neil watching her. Then he stood up and put on his jacket.

'I'll wait for you in the car.' His smile was warm, his tone intimate, suggesting they had known each other far longer than a mere eight hours.

Elodie picked up the tray and started for the door. 'What makes you think I've changed my mind?' she said over her shoulder.

In a couple of strides he was blocking her exit. He sighed softly. 'Elodie, why waste precious time? Such games are futile and not worthy of you.'

Her chin rose. 'Has anyone ever told you what an arrogant so-and-so you are?'

'Not to my face,' he admitted.

'Well, there's a first time for everything,' she retorted crisply.

His slow smile made her scalp tingle and her heart seemed to skip a beat. 'Oh, yes,' he agreed. 'I'll see you in a few minutes.'

As she opened her mouth he laid his index finger on her lips. 'Enough.' Though little louder than a whisper it was, none the less a command. He held the door open for her.

'How kind.' Investing the words with all the irony she could muster, Elodie sailed past him without a backward glance, but she knew the heat in her cheeks betrayed her agitation.

Fifteen minutes later she took off her apron and tossed it into the laundry basket. Pulling a primrose lambswool sweater over her pale blue shirt and cotton trousers, she went out into the twilight. Locking the kitchen door with her own set of keys, Elodie dropped them into her bag and sucked in a lungful of cool fresh air, incredibly welcome after the heat and assorted cooking smells in the kitchen.

She crossed the yard and went out through the open gates into the car park. Looking neither left or right, she walked briskly towards the nearer of the two exits.

'Running away, Elodie?' The all-too-familiar deep voice startled her and she swivelled round. 'Now who don't you trust? Me . . . or yourself?'

'I am not *running* anywhere,' she responded furiously, scanning the shadows, unable to see him, which made her nervous and even more angry. Then a darker shadow detached itself from a group of rhododendron bushes.

Elodie's tongue flicked across her lips. 'I am going home. Alone, and on foot. So if you'll excuse me . . .' She started past him.

'As you wish.'

His casual acceptance took Elodie by surprise. She certainly hadn't expected quite such an easy victory. 'Right. Goodnight, then.' She set off towards the exit only to find him in step beside her. 'Where do you think you're going?' she demanded suspiciously.

'To my car.'

'Oh.' Feeling a little foolish, she settled her bag more firmly on her shoulder and started walking once more.

Tossing some keys in his hand, he crossed to an expensive-looking saloon parked next to the entrance. 'You go ahead,' he called. 'I'll be right behind you.' In one smooth movement he had opened the door and was folding himself into the driving seat.

Elodie stopped. 'What do you mean?'

The electric window hummed down. 'I should have thought it was obvious. I'm going to follow you.' He turned the key and the engine purred into life. 'Off you go, then.'

Elodie stared at him. Was he serious? 'You can't do that.'

He sighed and shook his head. 'You really should know better.' He switched on the headlights. 'An attractive young woman walking alone on country roads at night?' He clicked his tongue in disapproval. 'I can't stop you, but nor can I turn my back while you take such risks. I cannot allow anything to happen to you, Elodie. Not now.'

What did he mean, not now? It probably didn't mean anything. It was just another of his attempts to throw her off-balance. Well, not this time.

'You've been too long in the city, Mr Munroe.' Elodie was scathing. 'Down here we haven't yet had to adopt a siege mentality. I've been walking these roads since I was six, and the greatest risk I face is tripping over a hedgehog, or giving a badger a fright. Besides——' She broke off. She had been about to say that she was perfectly capable of taking care of herself. But remembering how, clamped hard against his powerful body, she had been totally incapable of struggling, the claim seemed less than wise.

'Besides?' he prompted, his sardonic tone telling her that he had guessed both what she had intended to say, and the reason for her change of mind.

'Besides, the fresh air will do me good,' she improvised quickly.

'If it's fresh air you want, we can wind the windows down,' he offered. 'Elodie, I intend to see you safely home. Now, I can kerb-crawl behind you all the way, or you can enjoy the journey in comfort. We both know you're tired.'

'It's nearly ten o'clock, and I've just finished work,' she pointed out drily. 'I *expect* to feel tired.'

'Indeed. But this was no ordinary day.' His tone softened. 'You've been through a profound emotional experience.'

As a wave of heat coursed through her body, Elodie was deeply grateful for the darkness.

'Nor should you underestimate the physical effects of——'

'Mr Munroe,' she interrupted, amazed she could sound so cool and cutting when inside she was reduced to a jelly by the memories his words provoked. 'A profound emotional experience.' Her treacherous body yearned for his touch, those strong, knowing hands moulding her like living clay, exquisitely sensitive to his lightest caress. She longed to feel the gentle pressure of his mouth on hers; that one time had been so achingly brief.

She moistened dry lips. 'You have this unfortunate tendency to overestimate your impact on women. I hope you won't mind my pointing this out. It might save you embarrassment in the future.'

Exhilaration rushed along her veins. Maybe that would put a dent in his ego. On second thoughts, she doubted it. His was cast iron. But at least she had not betrayed herself. He could have no idea of his true effect on her.

'Thank you for your concern,' he said gravely. 'I'll certainly keep it in mind.' His eyes glittered in the moonlight. 'But I was referring to the fact that you nearly drowned.'

Wishing she were somewhere—anywhere—else, her shirt clinging clammily to her back as she sweated in an agony of embarrassment, Elodie could only stare at him, totally bereft of speech.

Leaning over, he opened the passenger door. 'Get in,' he said quietly.

Aware that to say anything at all would only make matters worse, she got in. There was dignity in silence, she told herself. He didn't *know*. He might guess, but he had no proof. Not unless she actually admitted it, and she'd tear her tongue out by the roots sooner than do that.

As Neil backed the car out of its parking space and swung it round, Elodie saw Steven opening the door of his own car. He glanced up just as they swept past. It was too late for her to turn away. She glimpsed the shock on his face. Then they were out on to the road.

That was all she needed. Laying her head back against the padded rest, she closed her eyes. After his forceful warning against her having anything at all to do with Neil Munroe, Steven was bound to demand an explanation. Not only about her accepting a lift; there was also the fact that in the pub she had refused to talk to *him*.

Her eyes flew open and she straightened up. What was the matter with her? She didn't have to explain herself to anyone. Whether she chose to accept a lift home, and with whom, was no one else's business but hers. So she had changed her mind. Why shouldn't she?

But *she* had not changed her mind any more than she had declined to talk to Steven. Neil Munroe had done both for her.

'I've arranged our trip for Sunday,' he announced, slowing to allow a Mini crammed with teenagers to squeal past.

'I don't know if I'm free,' Elodie began.

'Well, you're not working.'

'How do you know?'

'Bill——'

'Told you,' Elodie finished wearily.

'And I'm damned sure nothing is as important to you right now as your property. So I'll pick you up at nine. We might be late back so I suggest you bring a jacket or something warm. Oh, and wear trousers.'

'Any more instructions?' she asked caustically.

'You'll get those on Sunday.'

Fervently wishing she could think of a suitable reply, something crushing enough to wipe the bland smile off his face, Elodie turned her head away and gazed out of the side-window, pointedly ignoring him.

The car coasted smoothly to a stop and, before she realised what was happening, he had got out and was opening her door.

Elodie's heart quickened. What now? Would he insist on walking with her to the cottage? Would he try to kiss her? Could she stop him? *Did she want to*?

She caught her breath as he lifted one hand and removed the scarf holding her hair back. The thick waves tumbled in burnished profusion over her shoulders.

Lifting a handful, he let it spill through his fingers. 'Amber silk,' he murmured.

She sensed him lean towards her, and felt herself respond, drawn like a moth to flame. But he stopped short, his head barely inches from hers.

'No, not amber. Cinnamon, perhaps,' he mused softly, 'with maybe a pinch of paprika.'

She realised suddenly that he wasn't referring solely to the colour of her hair, but to her personality. She had kept her eyes lowered but now she tilted her head back to meet his gaze.

An odd smile twisted his mouth. 'Goodnight, Elodie.'

Startled, relieved, *disappointed*, she was so immersed in her own confused reactions that it took a moment for the irony of his voice to register. When it did, she flushed. 'G-goodnight,' she stammered.

He laughed softly, shaking his head. 'Let me give you a word of advice. Trust your own instincts. Don't make assumptions based on malicious gossip. You pride yourself on your independence, so start showing some.' He brushed her cheek lightly with his fingertips. 'I'll see you on Sunday.'

Elodie watched the car's tail-lights disappear and laid her palm against her burning face. She remembered Steven's words. 'Behind the charm lie the scruples of a shark. He's a man with as much feeling as a machine.'

Today she had experienced feelings she hadn't even dreamed existed. The last two years had seen her life change dramatically. But nothing had prepared her for this.

Trust her instincts? Which ones? On the beach he had looked at her with open desire, yet his kiss had been gentle and restrained, not the passionate onslaught she had both feared and hoped for.

Yet, relentless as a juggernaut, and without her even being aware that it was happening until afterwards, he had got her to do exactly what he wanted.

A ruthless businessman prepared to exploit her inexperience, or a man of integrity living by his own rules. Which was Neil Munroe? There was only one way to find out.

CHAPTER FOUR

ELODIE woke with a start, her stomach churning. She wasn't looking forward to the day ahead but she had to go. She had no choice. The one good thing about it was that, while Neil Munroe was busy trying to convince her of his dedication to preserving the environment, his attention was distracted from her cottage.

The most sensible thing to do was regard the day purely as a business trip—what politicians and diplomats called a 'fact-finding mission'. She would appear cool, calm and open-minded. Though hiding her scepticism was not going to be easy.

Neil Munroe might be a formidably persuasive man, but he was about to learn that she could be equally determined.

The alarm clock on the small chest beside her bed showed a quarter to eight. Elodie sat up quickly. She had better move, and fast.

It wasn't surprising she had woken so late. Unable to switch her mind off, she hadn't got to sleep until nearly two.

At five minutes to nine she dashed into the tiny bathroom just off the kitchen, frowning into the mirrored doors on the medicine cabinet as she made a final check on her appearance.

Wearing a close-fitting but comfortable pair of stone-washed jeans, a navy and white striped rugby style shirt and her canvas shoes, she had brought down her Guernsey sweater to take along for warmth. Though with the local forecast promising yet another hot, dry day it seemed an unnecessary precaution.

She had kept her make-up to the usual bare minimum, a touch of mascara to define her long lashes, and a soft coral lipstick which added lustre to her mouth and enhanced a complexion already glowing with health.

For some inexplicable reason it had taken her longer than usual to have her bath and do her morning chores. Glancing at her watch, she realised that if Neil Munroe arrived on time she wasn't going to be ready. And he was bound to be on time if only to try and catch her out and prove that very point.

Unwilling to waste precious minutes braiding her hair into its customary plait, Elodie brushed it quickly, and hunted in the cabinet for her tortoiseshell slide.

With the gleaming waves fastened back off her face to fall loosely about her shoulders, and sea-green eyes bright with challenge at the thought of the day ahead, the image gazing back at her was startlingly different from the one she normally saw in the mornings. Never before had she looked so vibrantly *alive*.

It was simply the prospect of a change of scene, Elodie told herself. She hadn't been further than the nearby town for months. A day out, even if she did have to spend it with Neil Munroe, was a welcome break in the routine. That alone was quite enough to make her feel she had champagne instead of blood in her veins.

Even though she was expecting it the knock on the door made her jump. And as she lifted the latch her heart was hammering so hard, it made her slightly dizzy. He smiled and she felt her colour heighten as his gaze travelled over her.

Freshly shaved, his thick hair still damp and raked with comb marks, Neil Munroe was also wearing jeans, which he had teamed with a dazzlingly white polo shirt.

Elodie breathed an inward sigh of relief. With no idea where they were going, she hadn't been sure her choice of clothes was suitable, though he had specified trousers.

'What a lovely sight to greet a man on a Sunday morning. On any morning for that matter.'

Elodie's heart gave an extra beat. But though she could do nothing about the blush that suffused her from head to foot she was careful to keep her own smile polite rather than warm.

Did he really think she was so easily won over? That all it would take was a few well-chosen words and she would be putty in his hands? She had spent the last twenty-four hours preparing herself for just such tactics. 'Tell me, Mr Munroe——'

'Hold it.' He raised his hands. 'Couldn't we ease up on the formalities? You have a beautiful and unusual name. I like using it. But it gives me an unfair advantage. And that,' he added drily, 'is something I'm sure both of us would prefer to avoid. So unless you want me to address you as Miss Swann for the rest of the day, you'll have to start calling me Neil.'

Why not? She wasn't conceding anything, and it did indeed put them on a more equal footing. Elodie shrugged with elaborate indifference. 'All right.'

'All right, *Neil*.'

'All right, Neil,' she repeated.

He grinned. 'I like the way you manage to invest it with so many subtle inflexions. Now,' he went on as she drew a breath to challenge him, 'what was it you wanted me to tell you?'

Her expression altered to a mixture of irony and innocence. 'I just wondered if any of your ancestors were Irish.'

For a moment he looked puzzled, then his mouth twitched. 'No. As a matter of fact my grandparents were the ultimate dour Scots. Whatever eloquence I possess comes from a total belief in what I'm saying. You look as fresh as dew.' He paused, his voice deepening. 'I'd like to watch you wake.'

To do that he would need to be with her while she slept. The implications made her stomach contract in a tantalising blend of excitement and fear.

His gaze held hers and, dry-mouthed, Elodie merely dipped her head, fervently hoping he would interpret her tongue-tied silence as cool self-possession. 'Shall we go?' she suggested briskly, turning away to pick up her bag and sweater.

'You don't have a great deal of experience of men, do you?' he observed as they walked up the path to the road.

Elodie stopped. *Was it that obvious?* Burning with anger and humiliation, she turned on him. 'That is none of your business and certainly not a topic for discussion, so if——'

Clearly taken aback, he broke in. 'Hang on a moment, I didn't say *with* men, I said *of*. There's quite a difference.'

Elodie stared at him, then swallowed, her anger dissolving like snow in spring. Of course there was, a world of difference. 'Oh. I—I misheard you.'

He rested one hand on her shoulder. 'Listen, I think there's something we should get straight. One of the reasons I'm taking you out today is to shatter this image you have of me as an architectural vandal with no soul. So it would hardly be in my best interests, before we even set off, to deliberately upset or offend you, now would it?'

'No,' she admitted reluctantly, avoiding his eyes, acutely aware of the warmth of his palm. He was a very *tactile* man. The need to touch, to learn through texture and shape, was very much a part of her own life and the driving force behind her love of sculpture. So she understood and accepted the need in others. Yet this was different. This was *him*. And all her senses were on red alert.

Not that he had been over-familiar in the physical sense, or tried in any way to take advantage. It was just that when he touched her every cell in her body was charged with a mysterious energy and she was drawn to him like iron filings to a magnet. In those circumstances it was extremely difficult to remain detached and objective. But it was vital that she do exactly that.

'So perhaps if you could relax just a little, and stop treating me as if I were a reincarnation of Genghis Khan, we might avoid any more... misunderstandings?'

Elodie recalled the beautifully tailored suit he had worn on Friday evening. Superimposed on the memory was a vivid mental picture of Neil Munroe wrapped in animal skins, thundering on horseback across the Russian steppes, brandishing a sword. Then a shudder rippled down her spine.

He might have adopted the camouflage of urbane sophistication, but his aims were the same: take-over and domination. 'Elodie?'

She caught herself. Such thoughts were not only foolish and fanciful, they were dangerous. 'Yes.' She flicked him a wary glance. 'I take your point,' she allowed.

Sliding his hand down to grasp her arm very lightly just above the elbow, he started up the path once more, drawing her into step beside him.

He confided. 'A fault of mine—yes, I know you find it hard to believe, but I do have one or two— is that I say what I think.'

Unlocking the passenger door, he held it while she got in then closed it and went round to the driver's side. 'I realise it might occasionally be less than tactful, but I prefer straight-talking, then everyone knows exactly where they stand.'

'Such frankness is highly commendable,' Elodie observed drily, 'provided you are as good at taking it as you are at dishing it out.'

Half turning towards her to fasten his seatbelt, he looked up with a grin that made her heart roll over. 'If you can't stand the heat, you get out of the kitchen.' One heavy eyebrow rose fractionally. 'I am flame-proof.'

Refusing to be drawn, Elodie settled more comfortably against the plush upholstery. 'So what's the other one?'

'Other what?'

'Reason. You said *one* was to convince me——'

'Ah. Yes. It's perfectly simple. I enjoy your company.'

Elodie shot him a frosty glance. 'Of course you do. We've known each other so long, and we're *such* good friends. Don't patronise me, Mr Munroe. I'm nothing like the women you're used to.'

'There you go again,' he sighed in exasperation, 'jumping to conclusions about me. Though as it happens in this case you're right. You are most definitely not like most of the women I meet. This is very much a new experience for me.' The corners of his mouth twitched. 'It's rather like trying to avoid multiple punctures while handling a hedgehog.'

Elodie felt slightly uncomfortable as she recognised the truth. She turned her head and gazed out at the countryside. All right, so maybe she was just the slightest bit prickly. But he could hardly blame her. Until the day before yesterday the name 'Munroe Developments' had signified a faceless corporation which, after subjecting her grandmother to pressure which had deeply worried the old lady, had then begun besieging *her*.

Yet there was something about him which, in the face of all warnings, attracted her to him. And, while that didn't make the slightest difference to her decision not to sell, it did mean that the longer she spent in his company, the more confused her feelings became.

As they headed towards the dual carriageway, Neil glanced sideways at her. 'What sort of day did you have yesterday?'

She stared out through the windscreen. On Friday night, despite her being mentally and physically exhausted, sleep had eluded her, except for brief spells of fitful, restless dreaming in which he had figured far too strongly.

Then yesterday her obvious preoccupation had provoked curiosity and joking comment among both staff and customers at the pub.

At the end of her shift she had gone home intending to work on one of her dragons. But her thoughts had been so full of him, and consequently her fingers so unsteady, she had made a terrible mess and had ended up scrapping everything she'd done.

She had gone for a swim but, because of him, welcome solitude had mutated into a barren loneliness she found hard to handle.

What sort of a day had it been? Every minute had dragged. But if he thought she was going to bare *her* soul he was very much mistaken. She might be naïve, but she wasn't stupid. Honesty was one thing, giving a man like Neil Munroe ammunition of that calibre was something else again.

'Elodie?' he prompted.

'It was very much like any other Saturday,' she replied. 'Busy, interesting.' She shrugged. 'You know.'

Irony tinged his half-smile and his eyes met hers briefly. 'It sounds just like mine.'

He knew. Elodie turned her head, concentrating fiercely on the passing scenery as her heart thumped against her ribs.

They left the dual carriageway and turned down a side-road. A few minutes later Neil slowed the car. As he drove in through the open gates, Elodie stiffened in her seat.

Her startled gaze darted from the wind-sock billowing in the warm breeze to the huge grey hangar. 'What——?' Her voice emerged as a croak. Clearing her throat, she licked dry lips and tried again. 'Why have we come here?'

Neil glanced across at her. 'To pick up our transport.'

'*What*?'

'You seem surprised.' He grinned. 'Elodie, I'm not running some small back-street operation. My developments are spread all over the south-west.'

She merely nodded, but her initial tremor of unease mushroomed into dread.

Neil parked the car and opened his door. 'Don't forget your sweater,' he said, reaching into the back for his own.

Fear fluttered in her head like a frightened bird. Desperately she tried to talk herself out of it. If she backed out now without giving him a chance to show her his projects, she would have no defence against his condemnation of her as a closed-minded bigot. What was worse, there would be nothing to deflect his attention from her cottage and land. Which would put all the pressure squarely on her.

Elodie clenched her teeth to stop them chattering. Too distracted to wonder what was in the wickerwork case he had taken from the boot, she gathered up her bag and sweater and followed him towards the reception area, a single-storey office block attached to the control tower.

Trying vainly to quell her rising panic, she was hardly even aware of the uniformed man in shirtsleeves talking to Neil. Then she was ushered out on to a wide area of tarmac. To their right, at one end of the runway, three small planes were lined up on the perimeter of the turning circle, bright and smart in their red and white livery, their black-painted call signs clearly visible on the fuselage.

But Elodie was seeing a different scene—scarred earth and crumpled wreckage. Identification had been a formality. They hadn't allowed her to see the bodies. The doctor had been very kind. Better to remember them as they were, he'd said. He had been right, of course. But what he hadn't known, and what had haunted her ever since, was that it had been nearly five years since she'd seen them and she hadn't been able to remember what they'd looked like.

'Are you all right?' Neil's voice jerked her back to the present.

'What?' She felt dazed and shook her head to clear it. 'Yes, I'm fine,' she said quickly, shivering despite the climbing temperature.

'Are you sure? You look a bit pale. Oh, lord,' he frowned. 'Do you get airsick?'

Elodie shrugged. 'I don't know. I've never flown. But I've never been seasick,' she added, then could have kicked herself for saying something so stupid and totally irrelevant. But Neil took it in his stride.

'Nor have I, though I'm told it's pretty terrible. At first you're afraid you're going to die, then it gets worse and you wish you *could*. Anyway——' he was brisk '—if you've never flown you're in for a real treat.'

She'd have to say something. Excuses were out. She'd have to tell him the truth.

Slipping his hand under her elbow, he propelled her towards the three planes. 'Morning, Ted,' he greeted the overalled mechanic who was climbing out of the nearest.

Her tension increased. It felt as though there was a coiled spring inside her and each step they took wound it tighter. 'Neil——' she began, but her throat was so dry that her voice was just a whisper.

'Morning, Mr Munroe.' The mechanic wiped his hands on an oily rag. 'The flying school's starting early today, so I've parked her over yonder.' He jerked his head sideways.

'Thanks.'

As Neil steered her away from the planes, Elodie glanced back over her shoulder, then up at him. 'We're not going in one of those?' Her voice was tremulous with a mixture of hope and relief.

He shook his head. 'No. Now don't you think it might be a good idea to tell me what's bothering you?'

She looked at the ground, moving her shoulders in a helpless shrug. 'I'm scared,' she confessed, her voice barely above a whisper.

Dropping the case, he caught her shoulders with both hands and turned her to face him. Expecting impatience, she had already tensed herself against it, but his tone was surprisingly gentle. 'There's really nothing to be afraid of,' he reassured. 'Statistically——'

'I know,' she interrupted, 'you are safer in a plane than in a car. Only my parents weren't. Theirs crashed. They both died.' Now she had actually said the words, brought the root of her fear out into the open, it wasn't as difficult to go on as she expected. In fact, strangely, it was almost a relief.

'They were on their way back from France with two friends after a day at the races. My father was piloting the plane himself. He loved flying and had held a licence for twenty years. He used the plane for business trips to the continent. He said it was

so much quicker and more convenient than com-
mercial airlines.'

'What did your father do? His business, I mean.'

'He owned an electronics company, Swann
Components. They made magnetic heads for tape-
recorders and——'

Neil frowned. 'Garrett Swann was your father?'
he interrupted.

Elodie nodded. Her eyes widened. 'Did you know
him?'

Neil shook his head. 'No. I knew *of* him, though.
He was one of the few independents left. What
happened? The accident, I mean.'

Elodie looked away. 'Apparently it was a combination of bad weather and the radio failing——'
She broke off, scuffing her toe on the tarmac,
blinking away stinging tears.

Neil said nothing. His hands warm and firm on
her shoulders, he simply waited for her to continue.

'It wouldn't have mattered about the fog if he'd
had a radio beacon to home in on, but——' she
swallowed hard '—he strayed off-course and
ploughed into the side of a hill. There were no
survivors.'

'When did this happen?' Neil asked quietly.

'Nearly three years ago.' Taking a tissue from her
pocket, she quickly blew her nose. 'I'm over it now.
It was just——' She couldn't tell him the worst bit,
the bit that haunted her still. She was too ashamed.
She had loved her parents. How could she not remember what they looked like?

'It was just——' she repeated, indicating the small
planes. Wiping her nose again, she took a deep
breath and put the tissue away. 'Sorry. I——'

'For God's sake,' he was brusque, 'you don't have to apologise. I should have realised.'

She looked at him, puzzled. 'How?'

'From the fact that you were living with your grandmother and not your parents.'

'I've lived with my grandmother since I was five.' Her guard down, she hadn't stopped to think. It was too late now to call the words back.

His eyes narrowed, but to her immense relief he didn't ask the obvious question: *why*? Instead he released her and picked up the case. 'Look, in the circumstances, if you'd rather not——'

And have him take her back to the cottage? 'No, I'm all right, honestly,' she cut in. 'But if we're not going in one of those, how *are* we——?'

Silencing her by putting his index finger to his lips, Neil guided her past the half-open doors of the cavernous hangar. There, on the far side, on a circular pad of tarmac surrounded by close-cropped grass, sat a small helicopter. The top half was painted dark blue, the underside and landing-gear cream.

'In that,' he gestured. 'Like any small light plane, Cessnas are great for a sightseeing flip up the coast. But you can't land just anywhere. So, unless where you want to go happens to have an airfield right next door, you've got problems. I much prefer a chopper. They are far more convenient. I use this one nearly as much as I use my car.'

'This is *yours*?'

He nodded.

'How the other half live,' Elodie murmured wryly.

His swift glance held surprise, quickly masked, then he shrugged. 'It's merely an aid to efficiency.

I can keep an eye on several projects at once, and deal with any problems immediately they arise.' He opened the door for her. 'Up you get.'

As he seated himself beside her after sliding the case in behind the seats she was suddenly aware of how much less room there seemed to be in this bubble than in the BMW that had brought them here. Though equally comfortable, the seats were narrower. The panels above their heads were covered with switches and indicator lights and behind them head-sets hung on yet another control panel.

She was gazing warily around when, without warning, Neil leaned across her. She quickly disguised her swift intake of breath as a cough, but could do nothing about the rush of heat that made her skin prickle and her shirt stick to her back.

Her nostrils were full of the faint fragrance of his soap. His head was so close, she could see each separate hair. Dry now, tousled by the breeze, it smelled of fresh air and the warm musky scent that was peculiarly his. Her fingers itched to smooth it back, to bury themselves in the thick springy waves.

As she clenched her fists he turned and their eyes met. She held her breath as a shaft of sensation arrowed through her, sharp, sweet, and unfamiliar. She felt suddenly shaky.

His gaze flickered to her mouth. 'I have to make sure your safety harness is properly fastened.' His voice was more a vibration than a sound.

'Yes, of course,' she whispered, and put her arms through the straps he held, looking anywhere but at him. In the confined space it was inevitable that arms and bodies should collide, the contact brief but electrifying.

'It may get a little bumpy because of the heat.' He sounded slightly hoarse. 'I don't want you rattling around like a pea on a drum.'

'No.'

His fingers grazed the top of her thighs and she bit her lip as he clipped the buckle across her hips and pulled the strap tight.

Lifting one of the head-sets with attached microphone from the hook, he placed it over her ears. 'Once I start the engine and the rotors begin to wind up normal speech will be impossible,' he explained. 'We'll have to do all our talking through this, OK?'

She nodded, and as he turned away to strap himself in she noticed that his forehead was sheened with perspiration.

For the next few minutes he was fully occupied, talking to the control tower and preparing for take-off. Elodie was more than content simply to watch and listen. Then, suddenly, the helicopter seemed to tilt forward slightly and they were airborne, banking round to the right as they climbed into the cloudless sky.

After the initial shock she unclenched her fingers and toes, and relaxed, held firmly against the seat by her safety harness.

'All right?' Neil's voice came clearly through the head-set.

Elodie nodded, gazing in wonder at the panorama below.

'Glad you came?'

The irony in his demand brought Elodie's head round quickly.

'I wouldn't have missed this for anything,' she replied with total honesty.

'Then I'll have to see that the rest of the day lives up to it.'

'That won't be easy,' she warned, peering down as they flew over the village.

His soft laughter raised gooseflesh on her arms. 'We'll see.'

She could hear him humming under his breath as they flew on through the bright morning.

CHAPTER FIVE

'THIS was one of my early projects,' Neil said, bringing the helicopter lower and banking round in a wide circle.

The development formed a shallow 'S' on the gently sloping hillside. On either side of the road, properties nestled in large gardens bursting with colour and bounded by bushes and shrubs. Any fences were virtually invisible beneath clematis, honeysuckle, or virginia creeper. The mixture of houses and bungalows was made even more diverse by the variation in colour and finish on walls and paintwork.

'It doesn't look like an estate at all,' Elodie blurted, startled.

The corners of Neil's mouth twitched. 'Exactly.'

'Those trees,' Elodie pointed at the oaks and chestnuts whose leafy branches cast welcome shade over the pavements, 'surely *you* couldn't have——?'

'You're right, I didn't,' he broke in, anticipating her question. 'They were there long before I started building. This was originally parkland belonging to the manor house. Over there. See?' He pointed to an ivy-shrouded stone ruin some distance away. Standing in an overgrown garden walled on three sides, it was almost hidden by more trees.

'What happened?' Elodie asked.

'It burned down about a hundred years ago. The family couldn't afford to rebuild and moved into the dower house and the lodge. They lived off income from the woods behind the park for a number of years but then were forced to break up the estate and sell off most of the land.'

'Why?' As she recognised the resemblance to her own situation, Elodie's interest overrode her determination to remain detached.

Neil shrugged. 'The usual reason, death duties.'

Her heart lurched uncomfortably and she flicked a sidelong glance at him. But he was looking out of the side-window and even when he turned back to check the dials and gauges she could read nothing significant in his expression.

'They call it inheritance tax now,' he said. 'A new name for an old Treasury trick of killing two birds with one stone.'

She ought to change the subject. This was dangerous ground, especially as she had no means of knowing exactly how much he had found out about *her* financial problems. But her curiosity wouldn't be denied. 'What do you mean?'

'It's obvious, isn't it? The owner of the land has already paid tax in his or her lifetime. Then whoever inherits the land has to pay tax on it. As the sum is often more than they can afford they are forced to sell, which returns the land to the open market.' He paused, then added, 'And that's not necessarily a bad thing.'

Elodie glared at him. 'Not for you, it isn't. You'll buy it and build on it and add a few more noughts to the fortune in your bank account. But what about the poor people who have lost their home?'

His glance flicked her like a whip. 'Aren't you over-dramatising? The tax doesn't swallow the whole of the value of the property. Take that

parkland for example. After he'd sold it the previous owner paid his tax then went on a world cruise
before settling in the Bahamas.'

'Lucky him,' Elodie retorted. 'But not everyone
finds it quite so easy to leave a place he or she loves.'

'My dear girl——' Neil's expression reflected the
irony in his voice '—most people who inherit
property have never even clapped eyes on it, much
less actually lived there.' He brought the helicopter
round again. 'I don't believe anyone has a *right* to
another person's possessions. If you happen to inherit something—a house, or even a piece of land—
you are damn lucky. After all, you have acquired
something you didn't have to work for and which
has cost you nothing.'

'But what if, because of this damned tax, you
can't afford to keep it?' she demanded.

He shrugged. 'That's tough, but it's certainly not
the end of the world. You are still——'

'Better off than you were before,' she finished
for him. 'So you said.' She turned away to stare
out of the window. 'How could someone like you
possibly understand?' she murmured tightly.

'And what exactly *is* someone like me?' he enquired. Stung by the undercurrent of amusement
in his silky tone, Elodie jerked round to face him,
her chin high.

'A man always on the move. Someone who
doesn't belong anywhere, who has no roots.'

Spoken without hesitation, her words hung in the
air, and Elodie's eyes widened as she realised exactly
what she *had* said.

A muscle jumped in Neil's jaw, and she sensed
a sudden alertness, a sharpening of attention behind
the unemotional façade. 'Another assumption?' he

chided. Turning his head, he studied her, his narrow gaze thoughtful. 'As it happens, you're right. I do live a very mobile life. But it has advantages.'

'Oh, yes?' Elodie made no effort to hide her scepticism. 'Like what?'

'This is a beautiful country,' he replied. 'I see more of it than most. And I'm always meeting new people.'

'And how many do you actually get to know?' she scoffed. 'Meeting new people isn't the same as being part of a community.'

'What's so wonderful about belonging to a community?' His tone was acid. 'If you happen to be in any way *different* you are an immediate target for curiosity and gossip. Everyone has an opinion and they don't allow ignorance of the facts to stop them voicing it.' He paused. 'Surely you must have found that? Living with your grandmother, not to mention being a talented artist?'

Memories from her childhood bubbled to the surface of her mind—of taunts from classmates, and grown-ups falling suddenly silent when she walked into the village shops.

Unwilling to admit the truth but unable to deny it, Elodie shrugged. 'That's just human nature. It's not limited to villages. People don't have to know you to be curious. Look at newspapers and magazines. When there isn't a disaster to report, they rely on articles about the lives of the rich and famous to keep their circulation high.'

'But don't you find such curiosity intrusive?' he pressed.

'Why should I?' she countered, deliberately suppressing the remembered pain, the desperate desire to fit in and belong like everyone else, the con-

viction that her parents' absence had to be somehow
her fault. 'I'm under no obligation to satisfy it.
Anyway, I'm so busy with my own life I really don't
have time to worry about what other people are
thinking or doing.'

'I see. So, except at the most superficial level,
you really have very little contact with the
community.'

With all the precision of a surgeon wielding a
scalpel, he had laid bare the huge gap between the
way she spoke of her life and its reality.

Shaken, but determined not to show it, Elodie
shifted on her seat. 'Is there some particular point
you are trying to make?'

'Not at all,' he replied blandly. 'I simply can't
help wondering where you got this idea that in
outlook and attitude we are such total opposites.'

'Of course we are,' she exploded. 'There's no
comparison. We have absolutely nothing in
common. For a start I don't go chasing all over the
country trying to force people out of their homes.'

His look of contained impatience made her feel
like a rebellious pupil hauled up in front of the
headmaster. 'Come, now,' he remonstrated. 'How
can offering you a substantial sum of money
possibly be interpreted as using force?'

'You don't understand at all, do you?' Elodie
cried in frustrated despair. 'To you the valley is just
a parcel of land,' she cried, 'but it's my *home*.'

'Elodie, several acres of trees, grass, and undergrowth is not a *home*. A home is by definition a
building of some description. Whether it's a castle,
a tent, or an igloo, it is a place of warmth, shelter
and safety. Somewhere to eat and sleep and store
your possessions. Those facilities may indeed be

provided by your cottage, but they are certainly not limited to that one spot.'

She glowered at him. 'You have no feelings at all.' What chance was there of finding any common ground with such a man? How could he possibly imagine their lives had even the vaguest similarity?

'Because I view a situation objectively I have no feelings.' He rolled his eyes, a cynical smile twisting his mouth. 'What a perfect example of feminine logic.'

'Oh, I see.' She smiled back at him but her voice dripped sarcasm. 'There's *your* way of looking at things, and the wrong one.' She snorted in disgust. 'You call that *objective*?'

She tensed, waiting for his counter-attack, already planning her response, justifying an anger that she knew in her heart of hearts was a cover for other more complex emotions she did not want to face.

The outburst didn't come, and his sigh of mild exasperation left her confused. 'Elodie, why do you imagine I have no great attachment to any particular place? People with artistic flair are usually gifted with intuition as well. What does yours tell you about me?'

His composure unsettled her, indicating a refusal to be side-tracked. So did his question.

'I—nothing,' she retorted, anxious that he shouldn't know just how much she had thought about him during the past two days.

His dark brows rose in mocking surprise. 'Are you saying you have *no* opinion where I am concerned?'

As they were both fully aware that she had been leaping from one conclusion to another since that first dramatic moment of meeting an outright denial was impossible.

'Oh, you made an impression,' she acknowledged. 'It wasn't particularly favourable, that's all.'

Using her left hand and making the movement as casual as she could, she scooped her hair free of her collar. Damp with nervous perspiration, tendrils clung to her neck. The air felt deliciously cool on her clammy skin. 'Still,' she added, 'I don't suppose you'll lose much sleep over that. I certainly won't. As I said, I have far too much going on in my life to waste valuable time on matters of no importance.'

Letting her hair fall, she shook her head, implying by the gesture that for her the subject was closed, and gazed with elaborate interest at the landscape below.

His calm voice scythed through the chaos of her thoughts. 'Between the ages of five and fourteen I went to eight different schools.'

She glanced at him but said nothing, realising that this statement was only a lead-up to the point he really wanted to make.

'My father was in banking, where promotion depends on willingness to make frequent moves. My mother believed that boarding-school, while providing academic continuity, could not supply the advantages of family life. I learned at a very young age that *where* you are is not half as important as who you are with.'

'That's easy for you to say,' Elodie flared. 'I'm not saying people don't matter. Of course they do. But you can't rely on them. They can be here one minute and gone the next.' She looked away, disconcerted by his frowning gaze but determined to make her point. 'That is why roots are so important. Living in a place where every stick and stone has a memory attached to it gives you something to hold on to. That's what *home* is all about. It's emotional security. To suggest the word refers simply to a building is ridiculous.'

She stopped, slightly breathless from the strength of her feelings and the force with which she had put them forward. Why was he looking at her like that? Something had disturbed his habitual expression of cool amusement.

Compassion? From Neil Munroe? Never in a million years. Anyway, the last thing she needed was pity, least of all his.

Her chin rose a millimetre, silently daring him to argue.

'You may have a point,' he conceded.

Elodie blinked, her eyes widening. Of all possible reactions, that was the last she would have expected.

He smiled and there was something different about it, as if he now had the answer to something which had baffled him. 'I came past the convent on my way to pick you up this morning,' he remarked.

Elodie was relieved at the change of subject. She had sensed the situation slipping out of her control yet, not understanding how or why, she hadn't been able to stop it. 'Oh, yes?'

'Mm. The nuns were enjoying a late breakfast.'

She glanced at him in surprise. 'How do you know?'

'The windows were open and through flying beer cans and clouds of Old Navy ready-rubbed I could hear a rousing chorus of "She'll Be Coming Round The Mountain".'

Elodie stared at him. She *must* have misheard. He *couldn't* have said... Her hand flew to her mouth in an attempt to stifle uncontrollable giggles at the shockingly vivid picture. 'That's *awful*,' she gasped.

'I know,' he agreed, deadpan. 'Someone really should——'

'No, I mean *you*,' Elodie interrupted, trying desperately not to laugh. 'You've no respect for anything.'

He sighed. 'No soul, no feelings, no respect. That's quite an opinion you have of me.'

It was plain he was mocking her. Elodie looked him straight in the eye. 'I speak as I find.'

Neil's grin unsettled her. 'Look down,' he directed.

Elodie looked. Below them was another cluster of houses and bungalows built on rising land above a shallow river which wound like a silver ribbon down the valley. Though they appeared randomly placed, the properties followed the curve of the land so that each gained the maximum sunlight yet was sheltered from the prevailing wind.

'Another of your projects?' she enquired.

He nodded but gave her no chance to make any further comment. 'How about some lunch? I don't know about you but I'm starving.'

The morning's nervous tension had given Elodie a hollow feeling in her stomach which, during the past hour, had been growing steadily more uncomfortable. 'I could do with a bite,' she admitted.

'You'll have to come a little closer.'

'What?'

'I can't reach you from here,' he explained patiently.

Elodie flushed. 'Oh, very funny. So where are we going to eat?'

'Relax, I've got everything organised.'

'You would have,' she muttered.

'I've chosen somewhere with spectacular views,' he announced. 'The food is excellent and the service personal without being pushy.'

'It sounds rather exclusive.' Elodie's voice reflected her uncertainty as she glanced down at her jeans and rugby shirt.

'Oh, it is,' Neil agreed. 'Don't worry,' he mocked, 'we won't be turned away. In fact, with any luck we'll be the only ones there.'

Disconcerted by his ability to pick up her thoughts, Elodie wondered how he could be so sure.

Fifteen minutes later she knew.

Neil had set the helicopter down as lightly as a feather in the shadow of a stand of trees, high on a grassy hilltop.

With the warm breeze ruffling her hair, Elodie stood, hands in her pockets, gazing spellbound across a panorama of fields, farms and small villages to the sprawling town and the sea beyond.

A little way behind her Neil shook out a rug and began unpacking the wicker hamper he had carried from the back of the helicopter.

'Lunch is served, madam,' he called. 'And you'd better get over here fast. I won't be responsible for my actions if I don't eat soon.'

'I can't remember the last time I went on a picnic.' Elodie sat cross-legged opposite him.

Neil glanced up. 'I wanted to make the day different, something special. Lunch at a pub or hotel would have been far too much of a busman's holiday for you.'

Startled, Elodie had to clamp down tightly on a treacherous delight. She could not afford to forget that, beneath all his efforts to divert, impress, and entertain Neil Munroe's prime objective was her land.

He indicated the array of foil dishes and Elodie's empty stomach gurgled as she feasted her eyes on the mouth-watering spread.

'Cold roast chicken, ham off the bone, four different kinds of salad, fresh bread rolls with butter and, to finish off with, strawberries and cream.' He handed her a plate, a paper napkin, and cutlery. 'Help yourself.'

'That's certainly a different slant on personal service,' Elodie observed.

'I'm a great believer in efficiency and energy conservation,' was his bland reply. 'I've supplied it. You choose what and how much you want.'

Elodie forked some of the sliced meat on to her plate. 'Did you prepare all this?'

'Good lord, no.' He sounded shocked. 'Why would I waste my time when there's always some willing woman who can't wait to do it for me?'

Her head came up quickly. As their eyes met she read pointed irony in his gaze.

'Aren't you lucky?' Her tone was honey-sweet. 'Well whoever did obviously knows their job. You can keep your caviare and quail's eggs. I can cook cordon bleu, but for myself I prefer something simple.'

Neil had opened the hamper once more and was reaching inside. The corners of his mouth flickered as he looked up. 'Have you ever tasted caviare?' He was openly sceptical.

'As a matter of fact, I have,' she retorted.

'And did you like it?' he enquired silkily.

'I'm told it's an acquired taste,' Elodie replied. 'Though why anyone would want to acquire it I can't imagine.'

'And quail's eggs?'

She nodded. 'They really aren't worth the effort.'

He held up a bottle, the dark green glass dewed with condensation from the cooler. 'What about this? I find it quite pleasant.'

As she recognised the label Elodie's eyes grew round. 'That's fifty pounds a bottle,' she blurted.

'Surely it's the taste that counts?' he rebuked.

'Of course—I didn't mean——' she stammered, and jumped as the cork flew out with a loud pop and the wine foamed into the crystal champagne flute Neil was holding.

Handing it to her, he filled another for himself. As he raised it in mocking salute she saw thin red lines on the inside of his wrist and forearm. 'Your *very* good health, Elodie.'

The healing scratches and the inflexion in his voice brought it all flooding back; their semi-naked struggle in the water, her near-drowning, her accusation that he was trying to get rid of her.

Warmth flushed her cheeks, and her lashes fluttered down as she inclined her head in tongue-tied silence and lifted the glass to her mouth.

But before she had even tasted the straw-coloured wine he stayed her trembling hand. 'Wouldn't you like to propose a toast?'

Though cool, his fingers burned like a branding-iron on her wrist. Get out of my life and leave me in peace, she cried silently. But if she were to give him even a hint of her thoughts, his attention would be drawn back to her land, and that was the last thing she wanted.

'I—er——' She moistened her lips with the tip of her tongue. 'I can't think of one right now.'

His gaze held hers. 'No? You're not usually lost for words. Still, perhaps I could suggest something suitable.'

'I've no doubt you could,' she retorted sweetly, 'but that would be cheating, wouldn't it?' She raised her glass. 'Cheers.' The chilled, slightly dry wine slid down her parched throat like iced nectar, sharpening her appetite to the point where hunger overrode all reserve.

Helping herself from each of the dishes, she began to eat.

'This really is a delightful change,' Neil remarked.

Gazing round, Elodie nodded. 'Food tastes different out of doors. Gran and I used to have most of our meals outside in the summer.'

'Actually, I meant eating with a woman who sees food as a pleasure, not an enemy,' he remarked, refilling the glass she was surprised to see was already empty.

'I'm hungry,' she admitted. 'And it's all very tasty.' She swallowed some more champagne, feeling deliciously relaxed. 'But do you know the best thing about it?'

'The company?' he hazarded.

She shook her head. 'No.' Her sudden giggle surprised her. 'Oh, dear, I didn't mean—that didn't sound——'

'It's quite all right,' he allowed, straight-faced.

'The best thing of all——' Elodie leaned towards him, wanting him to understand how very important this was '—is that I didn't have anything to do with it.'

'I thought you liked your job,' Neil said, helping himself to more chicken.

'I do.' Elodie waved her fork expansively. 'But that doesn't mean I don't enjoy the occasional break from it.' She pulled a wry face. 'The trouble is, the breaks come when I can least afford them. And once Iris comes back——' She broke off.

'I don't understand.' Neil turned the stem of his glass, still half full of the golden wine, between his fingers. 'Your father was a very wealthy man. Surely he left you well provided for?'

Elodie's smile was crooked. 'He did, and he didn't.'

'Would you care to explain?' Neil topped up her glass again.

'There is money, lots of it. But it's all tied up in a trust fund which I can't touch until I'm twenty-five. So how I'm going to pay this damn tax——' She looked quickly up at him. 'But I'm not going to sell,' she warned.

'So what other solution do you have in mind?'

'Steven says he's going to sort something out,' she said airily.

'Is he indeed?' Neil mused. 'And how does he propose to do that?'

'I don't know,' Elodie admitted. 'He says it's too complicated for me to understand, and that I should just leave everything to him.' She brightened. 'Perhaps he'll sell some shares.'

Her confidence in that solution swiftly dissolved as she recalled the snatch of phone conversation she had overheard. 'But it might not be the right time.'

'What makes you say that?'

'Well...' She shook her head. 'No, I don't think I should...'

'Elodie, look at me.' Neil's voice was soft but held a steely command she found impossible to disobey. 'Nothing you tell me will be used against you. You have my word.'

His word? And yet she believed him. Was she mad? She took another mouthful of wine. 'I learned, quite by accident, that Steven recently lost money on a share deal that went wrong. I don't know exactly how much but I think it was rather a lot.'

'Is that so?' Neil's eyes glittered like sunlight on ice, but his voice revealed only mild interest. 'Would you care for some strawberries?'

A little while later, Elodie put down her spoon and, after draining the last sparkling drops from her glass, lay back on the rug, stretching luxuriously. 'Oh, I *did* enjoy that.' Filled with a glorious sense of well-being, she closed her eyes and filled her lungs with a deep sigh of satisfaction.

The sun was hotter than ever. The breeze had died away completely and even the birds were silent. Something brushed her arm and with great effort she opened her eyes. Neil was stretched out beside her. Lying on his stomach, he was propped up on his elbows rubbing a blade of grass between his fingers as he gazed at the view.

As he wasn't looking at her, Elodie didn't feel threatened by his closeness. She studied his craggy profile for a moment. He really did have marvellous bone-structure. Even when he got old he would still be an extraordinarily good-looking man.

Slowly, almost lazily, he turned his head, amusement hovering at the corners of his mouth. 'Thank you.'

She gazed at him, uncomprehending, then realisation dawned. She had actually spoken the thought aloud.

'Oh, dear.' She bit her lip, embarrassment threatening her rosy haze of content. 'You mustn't think—I wasn't being personal,' she cautioned.

'No?' The amusement deepened.

'No, definitely not.' Lifting her head, she shook it vigorously to show him how serious she was. But the action made her dizzy and she fell back on the rug. 'It was purely an...objective observation,' she pronounced carefully, wondering why her tongue and her brain weren't co-ordinating as well as they usually did.

'You were speaking as an artist?'

She nodded. Thank goodness he understood.

'But sculpture is three-dimensional, not flat like a painting.' Rolling on to his side, he grasped her wrist.

Transfixed by his piercing gaze, Elodie was incapable of resisting as he lifted it to his face. He slid his hand over hers and pressed her palm against his cheek.

She was acutely aware of the firm texture of his skin, of the faintest hint of beard despite his morning shave.

'To look is not enough.' He turned his head so his lips were against her palm as he spoke. 'You cannot fully experience anything through one sense alone.' As he followed her heart-line with the tip of his tongue she caught her breath, shuddering violently as her eyelids fluttered shut.

Raising her hand slightly, he grazed the soft flesh at the base of her thumb with his teeth. 'You have to touch.' With one fluid movement he rolled over again, his body half covering hers, its warm weight pinning her to the rug. 'To smell.'

Panic shivered through the rosy haze as he buried his face in the hollow between her neck and shoulder, inhaling deeply. But as he lifted his head, his eyes cloudy and heavy-lidded, and stroked her tumbled hair back from her forehead, a different kind of tension gathered like a swelling wave in the centre of Elodie's body.

'To taste,' he whispered, and lowered his head. His mouth took possession of hers and the wave broke. Scalding heat flooded through her. With lips and tongue he teased, coaxed, demanded a response, and it was impossible to deny him. Excitement was a slow fire in her veins and the pounding of her heartbeat deafened her as his stroking fingertips laid a burning trail down her neck.

Pushing aside the open collar of her rugby shirt, he pressed his lips to the pulse at the base of her throat. She gasped and quivered beneath him, caught up in a maelstrom of sensation that urged her towards some goal she did not recognise but desperately wanted to reach.

With a wordless sound, his breathing ragged, he caught her face between his hands as his mouth sought hers once more.

CHAPTER SIX

ELODIE heard a faint shout. But it seemed a long way away. And her senses, already blurred by the wine and the heat, were reeling under Neil's voluptuous assault.

He tore his mouth from hers and it was like a wound. She had been kissed before, but never like this. He aroused feelings in her she had never even dreamed of.

She heard him catch his breath then curse softly and she opened her eyes. But, before she could focus, a cold, wet nose snuffled in her ear and a long, wet tongue slapped warmly along the side of her face.

Gasping, Elodie jerked sideways. As Neil rolled off her she saw that the intruder was an exuberant red setter with a silky coat the colour of polished mahogany.

'Get out of here,' Neil roared. 'Go on, clear off.'

Standing amid the debris of their picnic, the dog cocked its head, gazing expectantly at them with limpid brown eyes. The pink tongue lolled from an open mouth as its glossy sides heaved in and out like bellows.

Elodie struggled into a sitting position, startled by the wanton earthiness of her feelings. Her whole body was aflame with unfulfilled yearning.

To find herself capable of such abandonment was not only deeply shocking, it shattered her image of herself as self-contained and level-headed. Who was this stranger in her skin?

Wiping the dew of moisture from her forehead with hands that trembled, she pulled her shirt straight and lifted her hair free of her collar.

But there was no breeze to cool her hot, damp skin. The rosy haze had gone, banished by the ache of acute frustration. She felt jittery and keyed-up and perilously close to tears. Biting the inside of her lower lip, she forced herself to take slow, deep breaths.

There was another shout, nearer this time, followed by a whistle.

'Go on.' Neil gestured impatiently at the dog. 'What are you waiting for?'

Realising that no one was going to play, the setter bounded away across the grass and disappeared over the brow of the hill.

'I used to like dogs,' Neil muttered.

Saying nothing, Elodie leaned forward and, for the sake of something to do, began gathering together the empty dishes and plates. Her hair swung down like a curtain, hiding her flushed face.

Neil's hand fastened around her wrist. 'Leave those,' he ordered.

Knowing that her face mirrored emotions too overwhelming to hide, she didn't look up. 'It's all right. I don't mind.'

'Well, I do,' he rapped. 'Why don't you stretch your legs, take a walk, powder your nose?' It wasn't a suggestion, it was a command.

As she glanced up he indicated the trees, then pushed one hand through his already tousled hair and turned away.

Flushing, she scrambled to her feet. He was making it patently obvious that he wanted her out of the way for a few minutes. And she was glad to go. Coming to terms with the powerful feelings he stirred in her was far more difficult than she imagined. At least he hadn't made any cracks about her lack of restraint. She wouldn't have answered for her reactions if he had.

As she strolled towards the copse she gradually stopped shaking and the edgy, wound-up feeling began to subside.

She had had very few boyfriends. Those she had gone out with had soon grown impatient with her reluctance to go further than kissing. When she had tried to explain that the excitement they got out of it just wasn't happening for her they grew impatient and angry. They called her names and told her she wasn't normal. And she had begun to believe them.

Now she knew differently. Unable to respond to the self-centred fumblings of boys, and that included Steven, despite the fact that he was in his late twenties, she had melted and caught fire in Neil Munroe's arms.

He was the first real man she had ever been close to. What was more, he knew it. 'You haven't much experience of men.' She closed her eyes, sucking in a deep, shuddering breath. Why was fate so cruel? Why did it have to be *him*, the one man she could not, in any circumstances, afford to fall in love with?

She got back just as he was stowing the rug and hamper in the helicopter. He didn't look at her and his manner was distant.

'Right,' he said brusquely, 'in you get.'

Elodie bristled. If he wanted to pretend that kiss hadn't happened, that was fine by her. In fact she ought to be grateful. Had he smiled or said something tender, she might have been foolish enough to believe it had actually meant something.

'Neil?' She paused, one foot inside the helicopter.

He glanced round. 'Yes?'

'Thanks.'

'For what?' His tone was dismissive.

'Opening my eyes.' She tossed the words over her shoulder and climbed into her seat.

'Perhaps I'd better make something clear,' he said, folding himself into his own seat. To be suddenly so close to him again made Elodie's skin tighten. 'Contrary to popular belief, this is not something I do often.'

Elodie moistened her lips. They still felt swollen from the bruising pressure of his kisses. 'Helicopter rides and champagne picnics?' she enquired coolly, deliberately misunderstanding him.

His expression hardened and his remarks about disliking the games most people played echoed in the back of her mind. 'What else?' Keeping his eyes on the instruments, he continued the pre-flight checks.

'Well,' she began, 'if your intention was to impress——' She broke off, flushing at his ironic smile. Neil Munroe would not step one inch out of his way to try to impress anybody. He didn't need to.

'All the same,' Elodie said, 'as a sales pitch it does have an edge.'

He glanced at her. 'That's the way you see today? As a sales pitch?' His tone was completely neutral, giving nothing away.

'What else?' She threw his own words back at him and, though her tone was light, inside she ached. It was painful to think of his thoughtfulness, of her awakening, of this whole day as simply part of a softening-up process. Yet what else could it be?

There was no denying the powerful, almost violent physical attraction that arced between them. But deluding herself that it might have a deeper significance could only lead to heartbreak.

'Even so, it's been quite pleasant.' That was the understatement of the decade. 'Though it hasn't made the slightest dent in my determination not to sell.'

He shook his head slowly. 'You're a hard woman, Elodie Swann.'

'That's right,' she agreed flippantly.

The look he gave her mocked the lie. 'As far as dents are concerned, don't be too sure,' he warned smoothly. 'After all, it's early yet.'

Elodie bit back the cutting retort that sprang to her lips and turned her head to look out of the window.

'I'd like to ask you something,' Neil said as, airborne once more, they headed south-west. The cornflower-blue sky had paled to milky pearl and towering pillars of cloud were boiling up over the horizon.

'Go ahead,' Elodie replied, 'though I don't promise to answer.'

'Fair enough. I have to say I'm curious. You didn't lose your parents until comparatively recently yet you went to live with your grandmother when you were still a child. Why?'

'It wasn't that they didn't love me,' she said quickly. 'But I simply didn't fit into their lifestyle.'

'*What*?'

The force of his reaction triggered an automatically defensive response in Elodie. 'It was very difficult for them. My mother had spent years studying for her accountancy qualifications. When she married my father she left her previous employer to join his company. I don't think they intended having children at all.'

'But you didn't go to live with your grandmother until you were six, so——'

'I was five, actually. Before that I was looked after by a succession of nannies. I'm sure they were the best my parents could afford, though with all the profits being ploughed back into the company there wasn't a lot of money to spare.'

Elodie massaged her fingers as if they were cold, not realising she was doing it until she caught Neil watching. She clasped her hands together in her lap. 'Anyway, none of them seemed to stay very long. Apparently there was too much interference from the family.' She gave a wry grimace. 'They meant Gran.'

'Who told you that? Your parents?'

'No, Gran did. She was always totally honest with me. She was also very traditional. She didn't approve of my mother wanting to continue with her career after she'd had me. But my father insisted he needed Mother in the office. She was the one person in whom he had absolute trust and he relied heavily on her financial judgement. In any case, my mother simply wasn't a homey person.'

'How did you get on with them?'

Elodie studied the landscape below. 'I didn't see them very often.'

'But when you did?' he prompted.

'They tried, I tried, but...' Elodie's hands spread in a gesture of helplessness.

Throughout her childhood and early teens she had struggled to summon up a genuine interest in her mother's enthusiastic tales of boardroom battles, company politics, and take-over bids.

And she knew the smartly dressed, attractive woman, whose reed-slim figure showed no sign of ever having borne a child, made a real effort to understand her daughter's enjoyment of the domesticity she herself had always loathed.

But the unbridgeable gap showed itself in stilted conversation and glassy smiles.

Her relationship with her father had been no closer. Though he was kind, in an absent-minded sort of way, she sensed she never had his full attention. Even when he was talking to her part of him was always somewhere else.

'They couldn't help it,' Elodie said. 'Some people are just not family-minded. They had each other and the business. There wasn't room for anything else.' She shrugged to show she had accepted it long ago. He mustn't think she was looking for sympathy.

'So your parents had the double problem of getting your grandmother off their backs, and finding someone suitable and permanent to take care of you.'

Elodie nodded. 'Sending me to live with her solved both at once. I'll always be grateful to them.'

Neil's eyes narrowed. 'You really mean that?'

Elodie nodded again. 'I could never have lived up to their expectations.'

'What on earth makes you think so?' Neil demanded.

'It's obvious. The company was their entire life. But it meant nothing to me. I had far more in common with my grandmother.'

'In what way?'

'I've always preferred working with my hands. Gran bought me Plasticine when I was little and helped me to model animals and birds. As soon as I was old enough she taught me to cook and sew.' Elodie's eyes grew misty as she recalled the golden days of her childhood.

'We grew all our own vegetables and soft fruit. By the time I was twelve I could produce a three-course meal, make crab-apple jelly, blackberry cordial, and four kinds of pastry. I could pickle onions and bottle pears and my damson jam won a prize at the local agricultural show.'

'Rather a limited, old-fashioned way of life, wasn't it?'

'You might think so.' Elodie's reply was tart. 'I don't. Gran always said happiness for a woman lay in being true to her own nature, not in imitating men.'

'And you share that view?' Surprise lifted Neil's dark brows.

'Yes, I do.' Elodie wished she didn't sound quite so defiant. She didn't have to prove anything.

'Your mother obviously didn't.'

Elodie shook her head. 'I don't agree. I know we didn't share the same interests, but as far as she was concerned my father's needs and wishes came before everything else. In that sense she was very much a woman.'

There was a hint of cynicism in his brief glance. 'I admire your loyalty.'

Elodie barely heard him. 'Gran gave me a far better start in life than many people get,' she said softly. 'I've been very lucky.'

'The fact that you think that way shows what a remarkable woman your grandmother was,' Neil observed. 'I'm sorry I never met her.'

Elodie's head flew round. 'You could have done,' she pointed out. 'But you were too busy. Instead you delegated someone to write letters in your name.' She turned away. 'It's too late now.'

Her eyes brimmed as she struggled with a grief all the more poignant because of this man's connection with her grandmother's death. 'You'll never know what you've missed.'

'That's something I'll have to live with.' His tone was flat. After a few moments' silence he glanced at her. 'Why aren't you married?'

Her eyes widened. 'I *beg* your pardon?'

'Well, wasn't that the whole purpose of your grandmother's teaching? To make you an excellent wife?'

'There's no law that says I must have a husband in order to enjoy doing the things I like doing.'

'I didn't say there was. I simply asked why you aren't married.'

Elodie shifted on her seat. 'I should have thought it was obvious. I haven't met anyone I'd want to spend the rest of my life with.'

He gave a snort of derisive laughter. 'You can't be that naïve?'

'What do you mean?'

'Thinking in terms of a lifetime when one in three marriages ends in divorce?'

'The statistics are appalling,' Elodie agreed. 'But if you look at them another way they are saying that two out of three marriages *do* last.'

He shook his head. 'I'd call that gambling against heavy odds.'

'Which is why' Elodie said, smiling sweetly, 'I am still single. What's your excuse?'

'Excuse?' His tone made it clear he considered it unnecessary to offer excuses or explanations for anything he did.

'All right, your reason, then.'

Amusement lit his eyes. 'How do you know I'm not married?'

His question caught Elodie unprepared. She ran her tongue over her teeth to stop her lip sticking to them. 'My solicitor happened to mention it.' She felt as though she had just gone down very fast in a lift and was waiting for her stomach to catch up as Steven's words echoed in her head ...

'The very idea is laughable. A man like him wouldn't waste time or energy on marriage. When it comes to women, he simply takes what he wants when he wants it and moves on. No woman will tie Neil Munroe down ...'

His brows lifted. 'You were interested enough to ask?'

Realising denial was pointless, Elodie made her shrug elaborately casual. 'I was curious to know what kind of man you were.'

'And what kind of man am I?'

Elodie's gaze fell to his hands. Though large and strong, they manipulated the helicopter's controls with a lightness and subtlety that sent shivers down her spine. He had handled her body in exactly the same way, his touch raising every nerve, every centimetre of skin to an exquisite sensitivity that was almost painful.

Yet she could not ignore Steven's warnings, especially as she had already glimpsed for herself Neil's ruthlessness and implacable determination.

She looked up. Though his eyes gleamed with a blend of amusement and irony, she sensed that her response was somehow important.

Just for an instant she was tempted to be glib and facetious, to toss him an answer she could hide behind. But the impulse was fleeting, dismissed even as it occurred. How could she expect honesty from him if she was not honest herself?

Her tongue snaked out to moisten her lips. 'Complex,' she said softly. 'Capable of great kindness and equal cruelty. Sophisticated and manipulative, yet startlingly candid, though even that is an arrogance...' Her voice faltered into silence.

His face was expressionless, his gaze seeming to pierce her very soul. 'And do you like me?'

'Does it matter?'

'I don't ask irrelevant questions,' he answered obliquely.

Elodie looked out at the changing sky. The billows of cumulus had flattened into purple-grey thunderheads. She shivered, then ridiculed her twinge of unease. Though the pearly light had taken on a pewtery tinge, eighty per cent of the sky was still cloudless except for small puffs that looked like wisps of candy-floss.

'I'm not sure,' she answered slowly. 'Like' was far too weak and nebulous a word to describe the tumult of emotions he stirred in her.

'I usually inspire very definite opinions in the people I meet.' He frowned but she could see it was ironic rather than angry. 'I hope you're not simply being polite?'

'I wouldn't insult you by being polite,' Elodie retorted. 'I'm simply being honest. And reserving judgement.'

'Very grateful, I'm sure.'

'You're welcome,' she responded crisply.

'Here we are.' As Neil swung the helicopter round and down in a shallow dive, Elodie followed his pointing finger. 'It's called Woodlands. I finished it a couple of years ago.'

Elodie counted six luxury homes set some distance apart amid landscaped gardens surrounded by trees culled to admit light while preserving as much privacy as possible.

'The houses are built on a south-facing slope and were designed with the top storey set back from the bottom to allow for a balcony running the full width of the house. The owners can watch the sun rise and set all year round if they feel so inclined,' Neil said.

'They look like the kind of places advertised on the most expensive pages of *Country Life*,' Elodie murmured, trying to compare this development with the new estate on the edge of the village, and giving up. There *was* no comparison. 'How much would one cost?'

'To build or to buy?'

'To buy.'

'Upwards of half a million——' Neil's broad shoulders moved under his polo shirt ' —depending on the state of the market.'

Elodie's mouth opened as she swivelled round and he shot her a look which combined amusement with mild impatience.

'It's not *all* profit, Elodie. Quite apart from the cost of the land and the actual building, the people those properties were designed for have very specific requirements.'

'Gold taps and a jacuzzi in the downstairs loo?' she enquired drily.

'I'm talking about security. The house at the top is owned by a prominent politician. Next door is a well-known film actor. Further down are the chairman of an airline and the managing director of a merchant bank. One was bought by a pop star but he only lived in it for a month before selling it to a Saudi prince who wanted somewhere as a base during the flat-racing season.'

Elodie could feel her eyes widening.

The muscles in Neil's denim-covered thighs flexed and bunched as he pressed the rudder pedals to swing the helicopter round again.

'All these people are possible targets for burglars or terrorists. The very latest in high-tech alarm systems—everything from electronic eyes to heat sensors—are installed as standard. Not just in the houses but in the gardens and around the perimeter of the estate. These people are looking for more than a home; they want peace of mind.'

As Neil lifted the helicopter out of its circling pattern and on to a new course Elodie waited for him to say something about his plans for her own land. But he didn't. As the silence lengthened she glanced across at him.

'Aren't you going to ask me what I think?'

He shook his head. 'No.'

'Why not?'

'I don't need to. If you thought the development was a blot on the landscape you wouldn't hesitate to tell me so. If you find it pleasing to look at I've proved my point.'

Elodie's lips tightened. He was so... arrogant, so sure of himself.

A sudden gust of wind blew the helicopter sideways, and though Neil quickly corrected its course Elodie's stomach felt as though it was still at the back of her throat.

A jagged blue-white flash of lightning split the dark, tumbling mass of cloud in front of them. Moments later a menacing rumble vibrated through the helicopter and a gut-wrenching spasm of fear made Elodie clench her hands in her lap. Her mouth was dust-dry and she couldn't swallow.

Staring straight ahead, flinching as another lightning flash momentarily blinded her, she sensed rather than saw Neil's quick glance.

'There's nothing to worry about,' he reassured.

'O-of c-c-course not,' she agreed, not believing him for one moment. A storm about to break and they were inside a bubble made largely of metal, and everyone knew that metal conducted electricity. Yet he was telling her there was nothing to worry about. Did he think she was totally stupid?

There was a prickling sensation on her forehead, and when she rubbed it her fingers came away wet with icy perspiration. Terror loomed like a great black mouth opening to swallow her. It was taking every ounce of will-power she had to resist it, and she was holding herself so tight that every muscle trembled with the effort.

The thunder didn't just rumble, it cracked, drowning the muffled roar of the helicopter's motor, deafening in spite of her headphones.

Elodie gasped and shut her eyes, but opened them again immediately. There was nowhere to hide, nowhere to run. She was trapped.

Her parents had died in an aircraft accident due to bad weather. Now it looked as if she was going to suffer the same fate. She started to giggle. This couldn't be happening. It was coincidence gone mad, something out of a black comedy.

'Stop that.' Neil's voice was sharp. 'Elodie, nothing is going to happen. You're quite safe.'

She gulped hard, choking back the threatening hysteria. With all her heart she wanted to believe him.

As if to mock his words the sky exploded in a cataclysm of light and noise and the helicopter suddenly rocketed skyward, tossed like a leaf on the turbulent air currents preceding the storm.

Elodie caught her breath, her mouth opening in a silent scream. Then as, without warning, it dropped like a stone, a strangled cry tore itself from her throat.

Her gaze was fixed on Neil, watching his hands and feet on the stick and rudder pedals as he regained control of the machine. His movements were smooth and restrained. Then she noticed how his thigh muscles bulged beneath the tight denim, and the sinews in his powerful arms stood out, and she realised that those continuous deft adjustments demanded a strength and concentration that she could barely comprehend.

As another blue-white flash lit up the cabin he glanced towards her, the hard planes of his face sheened with a thin film of sweat. 'Elodie, I promise you we're not in any danger. But it will take us longer to get back and it's going to be rather a rough ride.'

'No.' Elodie's mouth had the metallic taste of terror, and the word emerged as a croak. She licked her lips, cleared her throat, and tried again, her teeth chattering.

'Please,' she begged, unable to hide her desperation, 'let's land. I'm sorry. I can't——' She shook her head, catching her lower lip between her teeth to stop it quivering.

He looked at her for a long moment, as if debating something with himself, then he gave a brief nod and altered course.

Elodie dug her nails into her palms and when, a few minutes later, he said, 'Not far now,' she allowed herself to hope that they would actually touch down all in one piece.

Relief left her weak and shaky. 'Where are we going?' she asked. She didn't really care as long as she could get out of this machine and on to solid earth once more. 'You know, I used to wonder why the Pope kissed the ground every time he climbed out of an aeroplane,' she said, her voice still tremulous and pitched slightly higher than usual. 'I understand only too well now.'

There was a hint of sympathy in Neil's amused glance. 'I don't think his reason is *quite* the same as yours.' Pushing the stick forward, he took the helicopter down and they circled over an elegant Georgian house set well back from the road at the end of a long, curving drive.

The house was surrounded by terraced lawns which fell away to a thickly wooded boundary. On

one of the lower lawns was a circular concrete heli-
pad. A slanting ray of sunlight shone through a
break in the lowering storm-clouds, turning all the
front windows to shimmering sheets of gold.

'It's beautiful.' Elodie peered out of her window.
'Is it a hotel?'

'No.' Neil brought the helicopter down in a
sweeping turn and, hovering over the centre of the
pad, he set the helicopter down as lightly as a
breath. 'It's my headquarters.'

Removing his head-set, he gestured for her to do
the same. With the engine switched off the rotors
had stopped spinning and drooped under their own
weight.

'You mean it's been turned into offices?' Elodie
asked, her voice loud in the sudden blissful silence.

Neil had been making entries in two log books
which he replaced in a pocket in his door. Opening
it, he swung his legs out. 'Only the ground floor.
The rest has been converted into a luxury flat.'

Neil was already lifting the hamper and rug from
the back. 'We'd better get inside before the rain
starts. Come and hold these a moment.'

Scrambling out, Elodie took the rug and hamper
while he locked the doors of the helicopter. Then,
with a look she couldn't decipher, he took the
hamper in one hand, her elbow in the other, and
propelled her towards the front door.

CHAPTER SEVEN

'I JUST want to see if any mail has come in,' Neil said, leading the way into a small but well-appointed office.

'But it's Sunday,' Elodie said in surprise. 'There's no postal delivery on a Sunday.'

She noticed a hint of perfume lingering on the air. Then her eyes were drawn to a vase of red carnations standing on one corner of the desk. There was something blatant about the vivid flowers. Elodie sensed there was more to their presence than the adding of a human touch to a high-tech office. A small pot-plant would have achieved that.

Neil threw her a dry look. 'I know new technology takes a while to catch on in Cornwall, but surely you must have heard of fax machines?'

'Of course,' Elodie retorted, turning her back on the flowers. 'We're not exactly stuck in a time warp. It simply didn't occur to me that *you* would need one.'

Neil threw back his head and laughed. Elodie's gaze was drawn down his thick strong neck to the dark hair curling at the base of his throat. She recalled how, plastered flat by sea water, it covered his taut belly and disappeared beneath his boxer shorts.

Guiltily she thrust the memory away.

'What does it take to convince you, Elodie? I am running a multi-million-pound business. The most up-to-date communication systems are an absolute necessity.' His teeth looked very white in the gloom of the gathering storm. 'Competition is fierce. Instant access to information is vital, especially as we have several projects in various stages of development at any one time.'

'In that case——' she began, and quickly broke off. She wanted to ask him why, if the demands on his time were so great, he was devoting a whole day entirely to her. But she already knew the answer. He wanted her land. For him today was a short-term investment against a possible high-yield return.

'Yes?' he prompted.

Elodie shook her head. 'Nothing. It doesn't matter.'

As she watched him stride across to the fax machine and quickly scan the sheets she felt weighed down with hopelessness.

How *could* he claim that they had things in common? It wasn't that she felt in any way inferior, but his life was on a completely different scale from hers.

Still holding the papers, he opened a door and beckoned Elodie to follow him.

This second office was much larger and contained the latest in computers and photocopiers as well as state-of-the-art drawing-boards.

Her attention was caught by the large coloured photographs adorning the walls, all framed and protected by non-reflective glass. They showed aerial views of various developments, some of which she recognised, having seen them that afternoon.

'Well?' Neil demanded, as she moved along them. 'Do I still qualify as the ultimate philistine?'

'Perhaps that was a little harsh,' she conceded. 'You have more artistic vision than I expected. And, though obviously the whole idea is to make money, at least you appear to give value.'

His eyebrows rose and one corner of his mouth twitched in a mocking grin. 'How generous.'

Elodie turned away, ostensibly to examine the rest of the cool, high-ceilinged room, but in fact to hide her heightened colour. When he looked at her like that her legs turned to jelly.

She tried to imagine the offices during the week, humming with concentrated activity as designers, architects and quantity surveyors planned and costed the transformation of more acres of redundant farmland into another caringly landscaped development of luxury homes. All under the leadership of this frighteningly charismatic man. Who did the perfume belong to? Who had brought the flowers?

Conscious of his following gaze, she crossed to a large table which held a beautifully constructed three-dimensional scale model of a valley dotted with luxury bungalows nestling in shrub- and tree-bounded gardens. 'What's this for?'

Studying the model, she heard rather than saw Neil's approach. He stopped just behind her left shoulder. So sharp were her senses that she could feel his body heat. The musky scent of his sweat triggered a flush of response in her own body and her heartbeat quickened.

'A visual aid for the district council's planning department.' His breath fanned against the side of her face as he leaned forward slightly. 'The land earmarked for that project borders an area of outstanding natural beauty. They wanted to be sure the development wouldn't detract from it.'

Elodie swallowed, not daring to glance up. 'And were they convinced?'

'Mm.' Neil nodded. 'Work on the south side of the valley will be starting tomorrow.'

With every nerve screaming at his closeness, Elodie stared blindly in front of her. 'It's very impressive.'

'Wait till you see the real thing.' Something in his voice brought her head round quickly.

'What? We're not going there today, surely? Not now. I mean, the storm——'

As if to add weight to her objections, thunder rumbled across the sky, making the windows vibrate and Elodie jumped.

His gaze held hers. 'We'll see it tomorrow.' He paused, his half-smile tinged with irony. 'When I take you home.'

Her gaze flickered to the model. There was something vaguely familiar... She looked up at him once more, her blood running cold as realisation dawned. 'That's *my* valley,' she whispered.

'One half of it is,' he corrected. 'The other half *I* own.'

As Elodie stared at him, the full significance of his earlier words struck her like a blow.

If he was taking her home *tomorrow*, then they must be staying here for the night.

It was impossible, out of the question. She opened her mouth to tell him so, and shut it quickly. How could she object when she had been the one pleading with him to land at once and not attempt the journey back to Cornwall?

'Did you say something?' Neil enquired, and beneath the silky softness lay cold steel.

Elodie shook her head.

'Then if there is nothing else . . . ?'

'I've seen quite enough, thank you.' She spoke through clenched teeth. She longed to accuse him of having tricked her. But she couldn't because it wasn't true.

She *had* been surprised by the superior quality of the developments he had shown her. But that surprise had reluctantly turned to genuine admiration. Yet if she openly acknowledged the excellence of his work it would totally demolish one of her reasons for refusing to sell.

'Then we may as well go upstairs.' He gestured towards the front door. 'The flat has its own entrance around the side of the house. I try to keep my business and private lives separate, though unfortunately that isn't always possible.'

What was she supposed to make of *that*? Elodie wondered as their footsteps crunched on the gravelled drive. Was he only spending time with her because, as Steven had cautioned, she had something he wanted? Or was it his way of saying he would want to be with her even if he wasn't interested in her property?

No wonder Neil Munroe was known as a hard businessman. He gave nothing away, and had a positive gift for keeping people off-balance.

She wished he hadn't brought her here. If it was a compliment, showing her where and how he lived, he was sure to have an ulterior motive. And with so powerful an attraction, yet so much uncertainty, the tension was exhausting. On the other hand she couldn't have handled flying on into the breaking storm.

Glancing sideways at Neil, she caught him watching her with the same unfathomable expression she had glimpsed several times.

The air was heavy and sultry, the rumbling thunder and occasional flickers of lightning adding to the electric awareness that crackled between them like a high-voltage current, dewing her skin with perspiration and making her shirt cling.

As he unlocked the white-painted door, Elodie shook her hair back nervously, freeing the damp strands from her neck.

She followed Neil up the wide, curving staircase, past tall windows that looked out on to sweeping lawn and towering trees, into a large high-ceilinged living-room.

'Oh,' she breathed, her eyes widening as she looked around.

A Chinese rug lay on the grey-green carpet in front of a white marble fireplace. On either side of a rosewood coffee-table two roll-backed sofas strewn with jewel-coloured cushions invited relaxation. An antique glass-fronted bookcase stood between windows curtained in pale green brocade. Gilt-framed paintings and groups of prints hung on the apricot-white walls, and in each corner an arched alcove containing a variety of *objets d'art* glowed softly with concealed lighting.

'Oh, what?' Neil enquired, amused.

Looking around her, Elodie shrugged helplessly. 'It's so...*big*. You could probably fit the whole ground floor of my cottage in here. And yet it's——' She stopped abruptly.

'Go on,' he prompted.

She glanced at him, wary, suspicious.

'Tell me,' he insisted.

She turned, surveying the whole room. 'All this space and elegance could be very intimidating. But it isn't.'

'You sound surprised,' he observed drily.

'I am,' she admitted. 'I certainly didn't expect such a . . . relaxed atmosphere.'

'It is my home,' he pointed out. His expression changed. 'What exactly *did* you expect?' he demanded curiously.

Elodie gazed around her. 'I don't know. But not this. Not the sort of place that looks like the *Antiques Roadshow*, yet makes you feel you could kick off your shoes, sprawl on the sofa with a book, or your favourite music, and unwind from the pressures of the day.'

'Why shouldn't I need to unwind, just like anybody else?'

'You're not——' Elodie shrugged helplessly '—just anybody else,' she blurted.

He continued to gaze at her, his expression unreadable, and Elodie felt her cheeks grow warm. Her wariness returned.

'You did ask,' she reminded him.

His slow smile made her heart flip over. 'That's quite a compliment.'

'It's a statement of fact,' she responded crisply. The last thing she wanted was for him to think she was trying to butter him up. Then she caught sight of the two dragons standing side by side on the centre shelf of the nearer alcove. Glancing at him, she indicated the shimmering sculptures. 'I don't suppose you've had time yet——'

He came over to stand beside her, and immediately her heart began beating faster. 'As a matter of fact I saw Giles yesterday. He's the chap I mentioned.'

Elodie didn't try to hide her amazement. 'How on earth did you manage that? I mean, so soon?'

Neil shrugged. 'I had to go up to London on some other business. I gave him a call and he asked me to bring the dragons with me. As I expected, he was very impressed. He's had this great idea. He wants to——' He stopped suddenly and looked away.

'He wants to what?' Elodie demanded.

'No,' Neil shook his head. 'I think it's better not to say anything until he's sure he can fix it.'

'Fix *what*?' Elodie grabbed his arms, feeling her own hands tingle as she sensed the strength in the corded muscles beneath the warm skin. 'Neil, for heaven's sake, you can't drop hints like that then leave me in suspense. *Tell* me.'

He grinned down at her. 'All right, all right, unhand me, woman.'

Blushing furiously, she released him as though she had been stung.

'Look at this.' He held out his forearms for her inspection. 'First scratches, now fingerprints.'

'If you don't hurry up and tell me,' she warned, glaring at him, trying to ignore the hot, breathless feeling caused by the laughter dancing in his eyes, 'I'll——'

'You'll what?' he challenged softly.

'I'll—chew a hole in the carpet,' she finished in a rush.

His eyes didn't leave hers. 'All that frustration,' he tutted.

Elodie's face burned at the deliberate double-meaning in his choice of words. 'Just tell me. Please?'

'Giles runs a very prestigious art gallery. He organises exhibitions for artists and sculptors whose work is becoming collectable. He's going to see if he can arrange a small stand for your dragons. Of course, he'll need more than just those two——'

'That's no problem,' she interrupted quickly. 'I've got several more at home, and I'm sure I'll be able to borrow back the pair I made for Bill and Iris at the pub. An exhibition!' Incandescent with joy, without thinking, Elodie flung her arms around his neck. 'Oh, Neil, thank you. I *never* expected anything like this.'

'Nor did I,' he murmured softly and, lowering his head, he covered her mouth with his own.

As she caught her breath he imprisoned her face in his hands. Her lips, already parted in surprise, offered no barrier to his gently probing tongue, and suddenly the lightning seemed to be inside her, tingling like pins and needles along every nerve.

His kiss deepened, grew more demanding, its urgency re-igniting her own need and hunger. The warm roughness of his hands, the pressure of his lips, the man-smell of him went to her head like champagne, with the same dizzying effect.

Clinging to the corded muscle and hard bone of his shoulders, Elodie felt something open inside her like a blossoming flower and understood for the first time her power as a woman.

The realisation awed and thrilled her. Suddenly it was no longer enough simply to receive. She wanted to meet Neil's male strength with feminine

subtlety, and give him the same pleasure and excitement that his touch kindled in her.

With no experience to draw on she relied on instinct to guide her. Loosening her grip, she slid her
fingertips over his neck and threaded them through
his hair in a gentle caress as her body relaxed,
pliant, against his.

But something was wrong. She felt him change.
As tension left her, so it grew in him. A split-second
later he grasped her wrists and pulled them roughly
from around his neck. Stepping back, he deliberately distanced himself from her.

Moist-lipped and heavy-eyed, dazed by feelings
too powerful to conceal, Elodie looked up at him,
bewildered.

His soft, almost inaudible groan didn't match the
harsh expression on his face, or the rigidity of a
stance that hinted at a fierce inner battle for control.

Releasing her, he turned away, crouching to pick
up the fax sheets he had let fall.

'Please accept my apologies,' he said formally as
he straightened up.

'What for?' Confusion clouded Elodie's mind.

'I shouldn't have taken advantage of you like
that.' He shuffled the papers into order, avoiding
her eyes.

'But you didn't——' she began.

'Yes I did, and it was unforgivable.' He glanced
at the messages once more, and his remoteness
pierced her like a blade.

'OK, I forgive you.' Elodie smiled at him, willing
him to smile back. She didn't understand what had
happened. The lovely warm closeness had gone. It
was as if he had pushed her out into a blizzard and
slammed the door in her face. But *why*?

'Neil——?'

'Look, there are one or two things I have to see to. Business matters that can't wait. Why don't you go and have a shower? I'm sure you'll feel more comfortable.'

It was only too plain that he wanted her out of the way for a while. And if she was not to make a complete fool of herself she would be wise to do as he suggested.

Every minute she spent with him made it harder to remember that there was no future in their relationship.

'Thank you,' she managed, her throat stiff with pain. His suggestion was strangely intimate, considering they had known each other less than three days. But the first dramatic moment of their meeting had warned her that Neil Munroe cared little for convention.

She followed him along the landing. He moved with the smooth grace of a prowling cat. Even in jeans and a polo shirt he had presence, a self-possession which set him apart and, when he chose, made him completely unapproachable.

He opened a door and stood back, refusing to meet her pleading gaze. 'Help yourself to fresh towels from the airing-cupboard. And take your time. There's no hurry.' He was already walking away as Elodie thanked him again.

Closing the door, she flipped the catch to lock it and covered her face with her hands. The tears she had been fighting welled up and spilled over, trickling through her fingers. Sobs racked her and her chest hurt with the effort of holding them in. But pride insisted she didn't make a sound. On no account must he know.

It was obvious that he found her physically arousing. *But that was all*. And, with no emotional involvement on his part, he had refused to take advantage of the potent attraction between them.

Elodie wiped her eyes with the heels of both hands. In spite of what the rumours said, Neil Munroe was, in his own way, an honourable man. But that did little to soothe the pain of his rebuff.

Because it wasn't just her body he had awakened. Love was a word she was wary of. She wasn't even sure such a thing existed, especially for her. And rather than risk more rejection she had shied away from situations which threatened her emotional composure.

Until three days ago. Until a cruelly ironic twist of fate had sent Neil Munroe into her life.

It was not a matter of blame. They each believed in what they were doing. But the valley was more than just home to her, it was her last link with the past. Leaving the cottage would mean abandoning the only security she had ever known. *She wasn't ready*.

Her head ached from confusion and hurt. A cool, refreshing shower might ease the feeling of pressure. Drawing in a deep, tremulous breath, Elodie wiped her eyes again and turned to look around her.

Glazed tiles of opalescent turquoise lined the shower cubicle and surrounded the huge bath. A toning carpet covered the floor, and thick white towels hung on a heated rail.

Kicking her shoes into a corner, she pulled the slide out of her hair and stripped off her clothes. She switched on the water, adjusted the temperature to lukewarm and stepped into the cubicle, closing her eyes as the needle-sharp spray washed over her clammy body.

A shelf inside the shower held soap and shampoo, both scented with the same fresh fragrance she had smelled on Neil when he arrived to pick her up that morning.

How long ago that seemed and how much had happened since. Anguish stabbed again, and she bit her lip hard. She would *not* cry. If she needed a reminder that emotion equalled pain, then surely this was it. She could not, *must* not allow it to happen again.

As she rinsed the lather from her hair, the room was lit by a brilliant lightning flash followed immediately by an ear-splitting clap of thunder.

The shock made Elodie start violently. Soapy water stung her eyes and she gasped. Shutting them tight, she swept the curtain aside. The smooth base of the shower tray was already slippery with lather and shampoo. As she grabbed for a towel, her balance already precarious, her feet shot from under her and, with a cry of alarm, she crashed down.

As she sprawled, winded and dazed, half-in and half-out of the shower, the door slammed back against the wall and Neil burst in.

Switching off the shower, he dropped to his knees beside her. 'Are you hurt?' he demanded harshly.

'I'm not exactly comfortable.' Elodie winced. Pushing her dripping hair back with a trembling hand, she glimpsed Neil's face, and was startled by his pallor. The skin around his nostrils was white and his mouth was taut with strain.

'I meant, have you broken anything? And I'm talking about bones, not the curtain or the shower tray.'

She made a tiny negative movement with her head. 'I don't know, I—I don't think so.' She rubbed her streaming eyes with her fingertips.

'You *are* hurt.' His voice was hard, accusing.

She shook her head again. 'No, I got soap in my eyes, that's all.' Why was he so angry?

'Are you sure?'

'As far as I can tell I'm OK. But I won't know for certain until . . .' She started to push herself up.

'Take it slowly.' Sliding his arm under her shoulders, Neil lifted her carefully to her feet.

'Aagh.' Elodie bit her lip. 'Sorry.'

'For God's sake,' he snapped, 'you don't have to apologise. Just stop trying to hurry.'

Catching her breath, Elodie gradually straightened up, mentally exploring her bruised and shaken body as she did so.

'I'm sure nothing's broken.' Gripping his arm, she reached her full height, light-headed from a mixture of shock and relief. 'I expect by tomorrow I'll be every colour of the rainbow, and so stiff, you'll have to fold me up to get me in the helicopter.' Letting her breath out in a shaky rush, she grinned up at him.

Their eyes met and locked. Seconds ticked by as awareness, recognition and memory flashed between them with all the dazzling speed of the lightning outside.

Elodie felt her entire body tingle as she flushed from head to foot. This was the second time he had rescued her. But now there was not even a bikini bottom to protect her modesty. Here she was, naked in his arms, only minutes after he had made it painfully clear that he wanted no further physical contact with her.

Oh, God, what if he thought she had done it on purpose? Elodie shrank away from him, her stinging eyes widening. 'Please,' she began urgently, 'you mustn't think——'

'What the hell is it with you?' he grated, not letting her finish. And his arm tightened, imprisoning her as she tried to pull away.

His eyes had a dangerous glitter and a muscle twitched at the point of his jaw. 'Have you got some sort of death-wish where water's concerned?'

'I didn't get cramp on purpose,' she blazed. 'And this fall wasn't a barrel of laughs either. Anyway, you shouldn't be in here at all. I locked the door.'

'Then thank your lucky stars the lock's broken,' he retaliated. 'What if you had knocked yourself out?'

'At l-least I'd h-have b-been unconscious in p-private,' she retorted, her teeth beginning to chatter.

'God, you're impossible,' he muttered.

As he grabbed the towel she was reaching for, his hand brushed lightly against her breast. They both froze. Elodie's sharp intake of breath was loud in the silence. Then lightning flickered, breaking the spell. And as another clap of thunder reverberated across the sky Neil thrust the towel into her hands, turned on his heel, and strode out.

Dressed once more, her hair rubbed so fiercely that it was almost dry, Elodie gathered up her courage and returned to the living-room.

As she closed the door behind her Neil emerged from what she assumed to be the kitchen, carrying a tray set with tea things, plus a plate of sandwiches and another of jam-and-cream-filled sponge cake.

Taking a deep breath, Elodie tilted her chin a fraction higher. 'Don't you...like me?' she blurted.

Putting the tray down on the coffee-table, Neil straightened up slowly.

'Please, I'd rather know the truth,' she said quickly.

Dipping his head in acknowledgement, Neil looked directly at her. 'The truth?' he murmured, so softly that she barely heard him. 'Yes, I like you. But that's not really what you are asking, is it?' He gestured towards one of the sofas and, as she sat, settled himself opposite, the coffee-table between them.

Head bent, Elodie fretted with a hangnail. 'You said I'm not like other women you've known. I guess by that you mean I haven't—I'm not...experienced. Is that why you won't...?'

Swallowing, she raised her eyes and met his narrowed gaze. His expression was unreadable, giving no clue to his thoughts. She had no choice but to plough on. She had to *know*. 'When you touch me, kiss me, it—I—and I know it's the same for you. You say you like me. So——' Elodie clasped her hands tightly together '—why do you push me away?'

Suddenly his eyes were glittering slits in a mask of anger. 'Are you serious? Haven't you learned that playing with fire gets you burned? You're no longer a child, Elodie. There's no excuse for that kind of naïveté, not from a grown woman.'

'Then why don't you treat me like one?' she flung back at him. 'I make my own decisions. I don't need someone else deciding what's best for me.'

Neil pushed his hands through his hair, the gesture mirroring his frustration, and smiled grimly. 'It seems that's *exactly* what you need. And, let me tell you, it hasn't been easy. I find you extremely attractive. There is something very special——' He broke off abruptly and Elodie struggled to contain her startled joy at his admission. 'But if I took you to bed now, how would you ever be sure I hadn't used that aspect of our relationship to pressure you into selling?'

'The two things are entirely separate,' she declared. 'In any case, I've already told you there is no question of my selling.'

Surprise lifted Neil's eyebrows and he shook his head, his expression perplexed. 'You certainly are different.'

'What do you mean?' she asked warily.

His lip curled in cynical amusement, but his gaze was perplexed. 'You haven't mentioned love.'

She moistened her lips. 'What's that got to do with anything? You've already made it clear that you have no time for the games most people play. Well, nor have I. And talking about love when the issue is physical attraction is one of them.'

Crossing one leg over the other, Neil leaned back, studying her, his eyes veiled. 'Don't you believe in love?'

Elodie shrugged, the movement a little too flippant, revealing rather than hiding her deep hurt. 'It would be stupid, not to mention self-destructive to believe in something which only leads to grief.'

Neil's eyes were twin lasers laying bare her very soul. But she didn't flinch, though her cheeks grew hot and the palms of her hands damp.

Uncrossing his legs, Neil rested his elbows on his knees, a frown creasing his forehead. 'And you think what you are proposing doesn't?' He paused, clearly choosing his words. 'Elodie, while a man is quite capable of separating sex from love, a woman attempting to do the same is likely to end up an emotional cripple.'

Elodie tossed her head. 'How would you know? You've never been a woman.'

'True,' he conceded. 'But I've had plenty of opportunity for observation.'

Blushing furiously now, Elodie tilted her chin a degree higher. 'Well, I still say the choice is my responsibility, not yours.'

With a regretful sigh Neil shook his head. 'I'm afraid I can't agree. After all, I would be very much involved. In any case——' the merest suggestion of a smile hovered at the corners of his mouth '—I don't want simply to be used.'

Elodie's throat was paper-dry. At surface level it looked as though she was being rejected again. But with Neil Munroe appearances were all too often deceptive. She tried to swallow, and saw his gaze flick to her throat. 'Wh—what *do* you want, then?'

Suddenly he relaxed and, leaning forward, poured milk into the cups. Replacing the jug, he glanced up and his smile sent darts of excitement and anticipation through her. 'You already know the answer to that. I want your land.' He paused, looking directly into her eyes. 'I also want you, but not on your terms. And, as I have already mentioned, sooner or later I always get what I want.' Calmly he lifted the teapot. 'How do you like it?'

CHAPTER EIGHT

AFTER switching out the light Elodie had pulled back the curtains as she always did at home. Lying on her back in the guest-room's vast double bed, covered only by a sheet, she gazed at the night sky through rain-streaked glass.

Thunder still growled, but it was fainter and less frequent. The rain had started two hours ago with single fat drops bursting like overripe fruit as they hit the parched earth.

With Neil at her shoulder she had watched the squall approach, a dark veil of water falling from the purple-grey clouds to the ground, rippled like silk by the accompanying wind.

By unspoken mutual agreement they had changed the subject and talked of other things and the shift from intensely personal topics had eased Elodie's tension. She had actually laughed until her sides ached at Neil's descriptions of the disasters which seemed an inevitable part of his family's house moves.

As daylight had faded into the dusk of evening the rain had settled into a steady downpour. But, curled up on the sofa listening to Neil, the curtains drawn and soft lamplight filling the room, Elodie had forgotten about it.

Now it sounded like handfuls of gravel hurled against the window. But at least it had cooled and freshened the air even if the noise was keeping her awake.

Elodie sighed and turned over, punching her pillow into a different shape. Who was she trying to fool? It wasn't because of the rain, or the distant thunder that she couldn't sleep.

'I also want you, but not on your terms... And... sooner or later I always get what I want.'

Neil Munroe had brought her to the brink of womanhood, but he would not carry her over the threshold until she acknowledged her true feelings. By which he meant admitting she loved him.

But how did he know she did? And *did* she? What was love anyway? A chemical reaction? A biological urge?

All right, she was forced to admit she liked him. She liked his dry humour, and the way he mocked himself as well as others. Also, despite all her expectations to the contrary, she respected him. He had high standards and refused to compromise.

They had clashed, certainly, but she had learned a lot from him. He had opened her eyes and her mind.

Financially they were poles apart yet they held remarkably similar views on what constituted quality of living.

Despite the inevitable tension she enjoyed being with him. Perhaps 'enjoyed' was the wrong word. The time they were apart she spent reliving every moment they had been together, and looking forward to their next meeting. And, when they *were* together, more and more she wanted him to touch her, to fill the newly recognised emptiness at her core and make her complete.

Being close to him made her blood sing. She felt *different*: vibrant, sensual, aware of all the subtleties of body language and eye contact she had never noticed before.

The one thing she didn't understand was his refusal. Surely the pleasure of a physical relationship with no emotional demands or hang-ups was most men's ideal?

Restlessly, Elodie turned over again. Neil Munroe was not like most men. She had sensed that from the start, and he had confirmed it several times over.

'I don't want simply to be used.' The echo of his words, with their undertone of irony, brought an involuntary smile to her lips. Wasn't that usually the woman's line?

She didn't want to *use* him. She wanted to share and give, as well as receive. She wanted to discover what pleased him and made him feel the way she had felt.

Was this what was meant by love? This wanting to be with one person above all others? To learn and discover? To be close, to trust?

Elodie sat up quickly. Pushing her tumbling hair back, she hugged her knees. Body and soul, she ached for him. It was only since meeting him that she had come to realise how lonely she was. It wasn't people she wanted—she was with people every day. It was one special person. Him. He had the power to release her heart from its cold, lonely prison. But...

What if she confessed, acknowledged the truth, that she *was* falling in love with him? What then? Her parents had rejected her in favour of their careers. Her grandmother had died. What if Neil decided he had made a mistake and he too walked away?

If that happened now, she could handle it. It wouldn't be easy, but she would survive. But, once she committed herself and said out loud what at the moment only she knew, there was no way back.

Lying down once more, Elodie turned on to her side, curled into a ball, and drew the sheet over her ears. It was a straight choice: safety and a lifetime of regret, or commitment and the risk of re-opening wounds which this time could destroy her. What was she to do?

Waking with a start, for a moment she didn't know where she was. Realisation brought her upright with a jerk and she winced at the soreness in her back and side.

She looked at her watch and grimaced. Tossing and turning until the early hours, then dozing only fitfully, she had overslept. It was twenty minutes to nine.

A loud rap on the bedroom door had her grabbing for the sheet, and she realised it was this sound which had woken her. 'Yes?' she croaked.

'Breakfast's ready,' Neil called.

'Give me five minutes,' she yelled back and crawled stiffly out of bed.

In the event it took nearly fifteen. Drying herself and getting dressed drew strong protest from her bruised muscles. And she had to grit her teeth as she combed her hair and fastened it back in the tortoiseshell slide. But she had no intention of facing Neil Munroe looking less than tidy.

Elodie pulled a face at her reflection. Though the quick shower had refreshed her and given her some much-needed colour, it had not erased the violet shadows beneath her eyes, or the fine lines of strain at the corners of her mouth.

It would be easier once she was back on her own ground with everything familiar around her. She would be sure then that she had made the right choice.

A haunted image stared back at her. 'Come on,' she muttered, 'you can do better than that. Where's your pride? Your spirit?'

Neil was sitting at the breakfast-bar studying a report as she walked carefully into the kitchen.

Freshly showered and shaved, his dark hair still wet, he looked cool, formal, and devastatingly handsome. Yesterday's jeans had been replaced by pearl-grey trousers, a white shirt with a fine red stripe, and a maroon and grey tie.

As she hesitated in the doorway, absorbing every detail of his appearance to store in her memory, he looked up and, after one swift appraising glance, pointed to the stool next to him.

'You look decidedly fragile,' he observed drily.

She started to shrug, which provoked an immediate protest from her bruised back, forcing her to abandon the gesture. 'You've probably got a lot to do today, and I don't want to hold you up so I'm ready to go as soon as——'

'Thank you for your consideration.' He inclined his head gravely. 'But we're not going anywhere until you've eaten.'

'Don't worry about that,' Elodie said quickly. 'I can have something when I get home.'

'Oh, Elodie,' he murmured, shaking his head. 'Are you really that anxious to get away from me?'

To her horror her eyes filled with tears. She started to avert her head but in a smooth, cat-like movement he was on his feet. He caught her chin and turned her face towards him. She tried to resist but he was too strong, and she had no strength or will left to fight.

She stood quite still, the betraying drops trembling on her lowered lashes.

'Look at me,' he grated.

She gave her head a brief shake.

'Say it, Elodie,' he demanded, his voice soft yet at the same time harsh.

Her eyes flew wide open and she wrenched free. 'You don't know what you're asking,' she cried.

He made no effort to touch her, but simply stood, his hands at his sides. 'Yes, I do. We both know you want to. Those three words are your passport to freedom. It doesn't matter how safe or comfortable you make it, a cage is still a cage. It's time to leave the past behind, Elodie. Time to spread your wings and fly.'

She felt as though she was literally tearing apart inside. In the early hours she had finally convinced herself that safety was the only sensible course. How could all this emotional upheaval possibly be *love*? She had known the man only a few days.

But just to see him, to be within his magnetic aura was enough to melt her resolve like snow in spring sunshine. When he looked into her eyes, the way he was doing now, his gaze stripped her soul bare, exposed all her most intimate hopes and fears. She had nowhere left to hide.

Something of her agony must have shown on her face for, reaching out, Neil took her arm and drew her gently to the nearer of the two stools.

'I'm sorry, sweetheart. I'm a selfish bastard and a lousy host. It's just that time——' He bit the words off, his frown quickly replaced by a rueful smile. 'You must be starving. Come on, let's have some breakfast. We'll talk later.'

'Must we?' Elodie pleaded. She was grateful for his consideration and thrilled beyond measure by the endearment, but all too aware that this was only a brief respite. It was not in Neil Munroe's nature to give up.

'Eat or talk? The answer to both is yes,' he said before she had a chance to say anything. 'Ignoring something won't make it go away.' His tone was firm but not unkind. 'Decisions have to be made, Elodie.'

Head bent, she rested her arms on the counter-top. 'I'm . . .' *Afraid* was what she wanted to say but couldn't. 'Not ready,' she whispered.

Lifting her hair with the back of his hand, he lightly massaged her neck. She caught her breath as her whole body responded to the warmth of his palm.

'I'd never deliberately hurt you.'

She nodded. She believed him. He wasn't a sadist. But nor would he live a lie.

'So, now we'll eat. And don't tell me you're not hungry,' he warned as she glanced up. 'I don't enjoy cooking, but breakfast is a necessity, so I've become quite an expert.' He squeezed her shoulder. 'The grapefruit is already prepared.' He indicated the fridge. 'If you'll get that out, I'll do the toast. The coffee is ready, and I've got scrambled eggs and bacon keeping hot.'

In spite of her bruises, and all the tension inside her, Elodie started to laugh. 'You really are incredible,' she spluttered, shaking her head.

His eyes narrowed to glittering slits. 'I'm much more than that,' he said softly, 'as I intend to prove to you in the not-too-distant future. But first things first.'

As Elodie took her first mouthful of crisp, lean bacon and creamy scrambled egg, she closed her eyes.

'That bad, eh? I am only an amateur, you know.'

Elodie swallowed. 'Mm,' she nodded, her tone dry, 'the way Crippen was only a doctor.'

Neil's eyebrows climbed. 'I'm not sure I like the comparison.'

'Then stop fishing,' she retorted. 'Compliments have to be freely given to be worth anything. And I was about to say, if I'd been given the chance, that this is some of the best scrambled egg I've ever tasted, and that includes my own.'

'Coming from you, that's quite a compliment,' Neil remarked. 'Maybe one day I'll let you into the secret. In the meantime, eat it while it's hot.'

'Yes, *sir*.' But she needed no further persuading. That first mouthful had made her realise just how ravenous she was.

'No, really.' Elodie shook her head as Neil offered her a third slice of toast. 'I couldn't. I'll burst.' She flexed her shoulders carefully and heaved a deep, contented sigh. 'It really was delicious, though. And you gave me heaps. I don't usually eat much in the morning——'

'Perhaps that is a habit you should reconsider,' he suggested, and drained his cup. 'More coffee?' He lifted the jug from its stand.

'I'd love some.' She saw him glance at his watch. 'Are you sure you have time, though? There must be things you ought to be doing.'

'There are,' he agreed seriously, 'but you won't let me do them.'

Elodie jerked round to face him.

'Careful,' he warned as she winced. 'Remember your back.'

'It's not easy to forget,' she muttered, gingerly swivelling on the stool. 'What do you mean, *I* won't let you? I was the one——'

'Indeed you were,' he interrupted with infuriating calm. 'But my choice of phrase was deliberate. The decision, the choice, is yours.'

As Elodie opened her mouth to reply, there were brisk footsteps in the passage outside and a female voice called Neil's name. But before he had a chance to answer the kitchen door opened.

'Oh, dear, I do apologise.'

'What is it, Fenella?' Neil enquired pleasantly. But Elodie detected an undertone of chilling anger that brought goose-pimples up on her arms.

However, the woman framed in the doorway seemed quite unaffected. Her cream linen two-piece and chocolate silk camisole had the expensive simplicity of a designer label. And from her smooth blonde bob to her Italian shoes she radiated sophistication.

'Good morning, Neil.' Her greeting and smile, addressed to him alone, were a tacit reproach.

And Elodie knew. There had been, maybe still was, something between Neil and this woman.

'I'm so sorry to interrupt. If I'd known you had a guest...' She made a vague apologetic gesture with one elegant hand, and Elodie sensed that it wouldn't have made the slightest difference—she would still have walked in as though she had every right to do so. 'We were wondering if everything was all right?'

Neil raised one dark brow. 'Why shouldn't it be?'

'I have been trying to reach you for the last twenty minutes. When you didn't answer——'

'I didn't answer because I haven't switched the phone through yet,' Neil said.

'I didn't know that. I was concerned. I thought you might have been taken ill or something.'

'How thoughtful, but as you can see I am in excellent health.' Rising to his feet behind her, he rested one hand casually on Elodie's shoulder. 'Elodie, this is Fenella Rowland, my personal assistant. Fenella, Elodie Swann.'

'Good morning, Miss Swann.' The woman inclined her head. But the practised social smile never reached her eyes, which remained unnervingly blank, like one-way glass. 'I hate to break up a party but there are one or two matters which require Mr Munroe's immediate attention. I'm sure you understand.'

Elodie started to get up but Neil's hand tightened on her shoulder, signalling her to remain right where she was.

'Crises this early on a Monday morning, Fenella? What's happened to your flair for organisation and management?' Neil's dry enquiry brought two spots of colour to Fenella's contoured cheekbones.

She drew herself up, and Elodie knew she would never be forgiven for having witnessed Neil's rebuke.

'This office runs like clockwork,' Fenella responded with icy calm. 'I can hardly be held responsible for other people's disorganisation. Mr Anderson has phoned to say he must have a decision this morning instead of Wednesday as previously agreed; the planners want a site meeting at Crownick; and Eddy needs to know if you intend to go to appeal on——'

Neil raised his hand. 'Point taken. I'll come at once.' He looked down at Elodie. 'Sorry about this. I'll be as quick as I can.' He gave her shoulder another tiny squeeze. 'Decisions, decisions,' he murmured so that only she could hear. 'They rule my life. If I'm not making them, I'm waiting for other people to do so.' And, before she could think of a suitable reply, he was striding towards the kitchen door.

Fenella followed him and as the kitchen door closed on them both Elodie started stacking the breakfast dishes. With so many demands on his time, doubtless Neil would want to leave as soon as possible. The least she could do in return for his hospitality was tidy up. Besides, if she kept busy, she wouldn't have time to think, to wonder...

The door opened behind her and she glanced round, surprised that he should be back so soon.

But it was Fenella who came in. Without a word she walked over to the breakfast-bar, picked up the report and returned to the door.

Fully expecting her to leave, Elodie was startled to see her close the door and lean against it.

The polished smile had vanished, and Fenella's expression was as hard as the flame-coloured enamel on her long nails as she hissed, 'If you think that by sleeping with Neil he'll give you a better price for your land, you're wrong.'

Stunned, speechless, Elodie could only stare at her. It wasn't surprising that Fenella knew who she was, considering the number of letters Elodie and

her grandmother had received from Neil's office.
But what really shook her was not simply Fenella's
assumption that she had slept with Neil, but that
she had only done so to get more money out of
him, an implication that she was little more than a
prostitute.

'As for any fond ideas you might have about a
future with Neil,' Fenella sneered, 'forget them. No
one will ever tie Neil Munroe down. He values his
freedom too much. In any case——' her painted
mouth curled derisively '—what could a country
bumpkin like you possibly offer a man like him?
All he wants is your land, and he'll use every
possible means of persuasion to get it.' Her mouth
thinned in a bitter smile. 'Neil Munroe could charm
a snowball into hell. I bet he found getting you into
bed a real yawn.'

Blushing violently, Elodie opened her mouth to
protest her relationship with Neil was nothing
like the picture Fenella had painted, that, far from
wanting *more* money, she didn't want to sell at all,
and that despite their profound attraction to one
another Neil had actually refused to make love to
her.

But one look at the other woman's cynical expression made her realise it was a total waste of
time. Fenella simply wouldn't believe her.

Instead, Elodie picked up the jug and poured
herself another cup of coffee. She was so proud
that her hand remained steady, it didn't occur to
her that her need to lubricate her dry throat would
be seen as a gloating snub. Until she glanced up
and glimpsed the venom in Fenella's eyes.

Elodie swallowed. 'I don't recognise the Neil
Munroe you've described. But if he is what you say

he is—a man who uses people and discards them
as soon as he's got what he wanted—why would
you want to go on working for someone so ruthless
and unfeeling?'

Fenella's finely plucked brows arched in disbelief
and a sneer twisted the flawlessly made-up face.
'Are you really that naïve, or just plain stupid? Neil
is not only gorgeous to look at, he is also very
wealthy and very powerful. Working for him is a
status symbol on its own. It also means I meet lots
of fascinating men who just love giving presents.'
She fingered one of her chunky gold earrings.

Elodie's shock must have showed, for Fenella
laughed. 'My God, you really are green. It's time
you had a lesson in reality.' She leaned forward,
her eyes sparkling like chips of ice. 'It's not love
that makes the world go round, it's money. Money
buys power, and power is the biggest turn-on there
is. A sensible woman accepts that. But a clever one
turns it to her advantage.'

Appalled, Elodie was saved from having to reply
by the sound of Neil's footsteps outside. Fenella
moved quickly away from the door and rucked her
skirt up above her knee. Extending one shapely leg
backwards, she half turned, examining her calf.

Bewildered, Elodie watched as the door opened
and Neil walked in. Fenella had placed herself in
such a position that her silk-clad leg was the first
thing he saw.

Hardly breaking his stride, Neil side-stepped past
his assistant. 'Another ladder, Fenella?' he enquired with cool irony. 'You really are unlucky with
tights.'

Smoothing down her skirt with a sensuous
wriggle designed to draw attention to the curve of

her hips and the outline of her thighs, Fenella
flashed him an arch smile. 'Stockings, Neil. You
know I only ever wear stockings.'

Catching Neil's eye, Elodie looked away quickly,
flushing with embarrassment at this sexually loaded
remark. She had been warned. What she *hadn't* expected was to actually come face to face with one
of Neil's mistresses.

'Of course. I can't imagine how a fact of such
earth-shattering importance slipped my mind,' he
rasped with a sudden cutting sarcasm.

Beneath her make-up Fenella grew pale.

Elodie held her breath. Neil wasn't just angry,
he was *furious*.

'You came back for the report. Have you got it?'
he snapped.

Fenella lifted the folder. 'I was just——'

'Then I suggest you return to the office and get
on with your work, which will leave me free to do
mine. Unless you have any other questions?'

'No.' Fenella's half-smile was polite and demure.
'Everything is quite clear now.' She turned her cold,
blank gaze on Elodie and gave a brief nod. 'Miss
Swann.'

Having been through so much emotional upheaval herself, Elodie was acutely sensitive to strong
emotion in others. Behind the expressionless façade
Fenella was shocked and angry at the way Neil had
spoken to her.

What had made him so cross?

'Fenella is a brilliant PA,' Neil remarked after
she had gone. 'I would not have kept her on
otherwise.'

Otherwise? Typically, he was not denying his
affair with Fenella. But what he had not made clear

was how things stood between them now. And that was one question Elodie could not, *would* not ask.

'She's the kind of woman who doesn't think of sex solely as a token of love or affection.' Though one corner of his mouth tilted upwards, there was no humour in his expression. 'Fenella also sees it as a means of buying or repaying favours.'

Elodie's head snapped up, her eyes widening in confusion and dismay. 'Are you suggesting——? You surely don't think that I——?'

'Of course I don't,' he retorted angrily. 'In spite of your desperate attempts to prove otherwise, you are a sensitive and emotional woman. Far too sensitive and emotional ever to resort to bartering your body.'

Elodie stared at him, overwhelming relief followed by shock at his insight.

'You keep doing that,' she blurted.

His dark brows climbed. 'Doing what?'

'Making statements about me. You're so definite, so sure of what you're saying. But we only met a few days ago. You can't possibly know me well enough to——'

'Who says I can't?' he responded, his eyes gleaming. 'Haven't you heard the old saying about the outsider seeing most of the game? Elodie, there are times when I'm sure I know you better than you know yourself.'

'That's exactly what I mean.' She raised her hands in frustration. 'Don't you think you are being ever so slightly patronising?'

'Probably,' he agreed. 'But that, and my *arrogance* are all part of my charm and fascination.'

Elodie raised her eyes to the ceiling. 'This is hopeless.'

'On the contrary' he countered swiftly. 'Not only do I have high hopes, I also have a great deal of determination. Which is why, as anyone who knows me will tell you——'

'You always get what you want in the end,' Elodie finished for him. 'So you've said, many times. In fact, you seem to think that, if you say it often enough, whatever you want will actually happen.'

Neil's hooded smile set her nerves quivering. 'I *know* it will, sweetheart. And I'm not just thinking of what's best for me.'

'Oh, I see. You've got *my* interests at heart,' Elodie glared at him, hopelessly torn.

'Yes, as a matter of fact I have,' he answered quietly.

He shouldn't say things like that. It was cruel. The words were balm to her bruised soul. And she wanted with all her heart to believe him. But first Steven, and now Fenella, had warned her. Even Neil himself had made no secret of his determination to have his own way.

'Why should you care what happens to me?' she challenged. 'I'm not important to you, not as a person, only as the owner of something you want. According to Fenella, I'm naïve and stupid.'

'You would be if you followed her example,' Neil retorted brusquely. 'Fenella has squandered a woman's greatest gift. As far as the company is concerned she has been a great asset. And she is, on the surface, an attractive, intelligent, sophisticated woman.'

Elodie winced and sighed, spreading her hands as she looked down at her own slender jean-clad figure. 'And I'm a very ordinary, very unsophisticated country girl——'

'Ordinary?' Neil snorted. 'You are nothing of the kind. And you are not listening. I said on the surface. Men sleep with women like Fenella, they take them on holidays, buy them presents. They wear them like a badge. But they don't marry them.'

Elodie stared at him blankly. 'What's marriage got to do with it?'

'Even in these liberated times it's still the ultimate security for a woman,' Neil stated.

About to make a caustic retort about the divorce statistics and the ability of women to earn their own living, Elodie didn't get the chance.

'I'm talking about *emotional* security,' Neil added, seeming, once again, to read her mind. 'Most men have mixed feelings about marriage. They see it as a haven and a trap, release from the hassle of hunting for a mate, and a restriction on their freedom.'

'So if a man asks her to marry him, a woman should be grateful for his sacrifice?' Elodie's voice had an edge.

'That's not quite how I'd have put it,' Neil said drily. 'Presumably her reactions would depend very much on how she felt about him. The point I am making is that, whereas a woman is basically monogamous, a man isn't.' He raised his hand before she could interrupt. 'We are talking biology, not choice.' His mouth quirked in a sardonic grin. 'Nature's little joke ensuring that since the beginning of time men and women have stormed out of caves, castles, mud huts or igloos, yelling, "I just don't understand you."'

Elodie couldn't help grinning back but she was still puzzled. 'I still don't see what this has to do with Fenella.'

Picking up his suit jacket from the end of the breakfast-bar, Neil put it on. 'Look at her lifestyle. She has a job she is good at, she travels, meets lots of people. She owns property, drives a car that enhances her image, and has several prominent men among her admirers. Sounds great, doesn't it? Freedom to please herself. To do what she wants, when she wants, with whom she wants, and no emotional strings to complicate matters.'

Elodie made a wistful face. 'The ideal bachelor existence.'

'Exactly. Equality in action.' Neil's gaze held her captive. 'So why,' he demanded softly, 'the leg show?'

Elodie stared at him. What was he saying? Suddenly Fenella's verbal attack on her the moment Neil had left the room sprang into her mind. As she replayed the words, realisation dawned.

She couldn't believe it at first. It seemed too ridiculous. Fenella, jealous? *Of her*? But what had that to do with all that stuff about marriage?

She pressed her fingertips to her temples. 'I don't understand.'

Neil smiled grimly. 'Don't worry, you will. Now it's time we were moving. We both have work waiting for us.'

Neil didn't talk much during the flight. But with so much on her mind Elodie was glad of the silence. The sun was shining, the air fresh and cool after the storm. And the views from the helicopter were spectacular.

But after the first few minutes Elodie no longer saw them as her thoughts turned inwards.

Neil had gone to great lengths to point out the differences between herself and Fenella. But what he hadn't said was whether his affair with her was over.

Clearly Fenella had been part of his life for years. As well as the personal aspect of their relationship, they had the added bond of working together.

She couldn't possibly compete with that. Neil's attentiveness to her had to be because he wanted her land.

Yet no matter how hard, how fiercely she tried to deny it, the hope that Neil's interest in her wasn't *entirely* based on business stubbornly refused to die.

CHAPTER NINE

As THEY touched down on the airfield Elodie was surprised to see it looking exactly the same as when they left. So much had happened to her in the past twenty-four hours that somehow she expected everything to have changed.

Neil glanced sideways at her. 'What are you smiling at?'

'Myself,' Elodie admitted wryly. 'I really am a total idiot sometimes.'

'No,' Neil shook his head, looking thoughtful. 'I wouldn't say *total*. Though with a bit more practice you might—ouch!' he grinned as Elodie thumped him in the ribs.

'I *am* sorry,' she cooed. 'My elbow must have slipped.'

'The passenger's code of conduct states that beating up the pilot is just not on,' he announced, sliding the log-books into their pouch and removing his head-set.

'Then the pilot shouldn't ask for it,' Elodie retorted, half turning towards him so that she could hang up her own earphones.

'There are penalties, you know,' he warned, the gleam in his narrowed eyes making her feel quivery inside.

'Oh, really?' Elodie was aiming for irony, but with his gaze skewering her like a butterfly on a pin and her heartbeat quickening by the second her tone wasn't at all what she had intended. Instead she sounded both nervous and eager.

Trying to regain control of her treacherous responses and of the situation, Elodie raised one eyebrow. She'd go for scepticism. 'Such as?'

His slow smile made her breath catch in her throat. Then, before she could move, his hand cupped the back of her head and his mouth was on hers.

Warm and gentle, his lips moved on hers with a subtle delicacy that forced a soft, wordless sound from her throat as excitement raced like tiny flames along every nerve, flooding her body with heat.

He raised his head. 'In matters of discipline,' he murmured, his voice slightly hoarse, 'the pilot has discretion.'

Elodie swallowed; she felt dizzy, as if her body didn't belong to her. '*He* chooses the punishment?'

She ran her tongue over her lips. The taste of him lingered and she wanted more. She saw his eyes follow the movement. 'Can I appeal?'

Desire hardened his features. 'You do,' he whispered, 'God knows you do.' Then, with obvious reluctance, he released her but still held her gaze. 'There isn't time right now to explore the situation as fully as I would like. However, you may be sure that the moment circumstances permit it will have my full and undivided attention.'

While his choice of words and tone of voice were formal and businesslike, the expression in his eyes made Elodie melt, and she shivered in delicious anticipation tinged with a *frisson* of fear.

Carrying the rug, she followed Neil through the airport reception area and out to the car park. Unsure whether the goose-pimples on her arms were

due to nervous tension or the new freshness in the
air, Elodie was glad of her warm sweater.

As they turned out on to the road, the car phone
buzzed softly. It was the first of several calls. Neil
listened more than he talked. His questions were
brief, his replies even briefer. But, during the drive
from the airport to the road where the lane led down
to her cottage, Elodie began to realise just how
complex Neil's business interests were.

As they reached the lane he had to pull up on to
the verge to allow two heavy lorries loaded with
hard core to pass, clouding the air with dust and
exhaust fumes.

Elodie watched them disappear round the bend,
a brown mud-slick on the road evidence of several
journeys already made. 'They must have started
early,' she remarked, her voice carefully
expressionless.

Neil's gaze was level and unflinching. 'Time is
money, especially on a project this size. That storm
last night might well mean we're in for a spell of
unsettled weather. The foreman will want to get
foundations laid before the site becomes a bog.' He
opened his door.

'You needn't get out,' Elodie said quickly,
slinging her bag over her shoulder. Opening her
door, she could hear the roar of bulldozers and
diggers over the brow of the hill. They might be
out of sight of the valley, but there would be no
escaping their presence.

She frowned, sniffing the air and looking round.
'Something's burning.'

Neil slammed his door and came round the front
of the car to join her. 'They're clearing the under-

growth and burning it on site. It saves time.' The
car phone buzzed but this time he ignored it.

'And time is money,' Elodie quoted back at him.
'Aren't you going to answer that?'

'I'm going to walk you home.'

'You don't have to,' she began. 'I've already
taken up far too much of your valuable time——'

'Surely that's for me to say?' he reproved gently.
'Don't go all prickly on me, Elodie.'

'What do you expect?' she cried. Then, like a
dam bursting, all her renewed fear and confusion
tumbled out. 'I've had the most wonderful time in
my life, except for——' She broke off abruptly and
Fenella's presence hung in the air between them like
a ghost.

Elodie dragged in a shaky breath, determinedly
thrusting her fears aside. 'And I come back to this.'
She flung her arm out, pointing in the direction of
the smoke. 'When will they reach the valley? This
week? Next? I know you've offered me a fair price.
I know your developments are far better than I ever
imagined. But this is my home and I don't want to
leave.

'Look,' she said in desperation, 'the pub restaurant is closed on Monday evenings so I'm not
working tonight. Come and have a meal here with
me. You showed me your work, your way of life.
Let me show you mine. Then maybe you'll understand why the valley means so much to me.'

Neil laid one hand lightly against the side of her
face and looked deep into her eyes. 'I understand
far better than you think. Thank you for the in-
vitation.' He stepped back.

Elodie searched his face. What did he mean?
'You will come?'

He nodded. 'I should be delighted.' He turned to go, half raising one hand in farewell. 'Until this evening, then.'

Elodie moved about the pub kitchen in a daze, still feeling the warm imprint of Neil's palm on her cheek. She organised her three helpers, smiled vaguely at their jokes, ignored their nudge-nudge questions and somehow managed to have all the food prepared and ready for serving as the lunchtime rush started. Then for the next two hours she worked on automatic pilot, only one coherent thought in her head. What had he meant, he understood far better than she thought? How could he? He had openly admitted that places were of little importance to him. It was people who mattered. Fenella?

At half-past two, just as Elodie was getting ready to leave, Bill came into the kitchen.

'Everything under control here?' He beamed, rubbing his hands as he made thc customary enquiry. Receiving the usual chorus of assent, he nodded. 'Good, good.' The he turned to Elodie. 'I'm off to see Iris. She says Betty has been marvellous. She's never been looked after so well. But she can't wait to come home, put her apron on, and get back into her own kitchen.'

Elodie forced a smile. Iris's return would put her out of a job. Yet, knowing how much Bill loved and missed his wife, how could she wish her to stay away longer?

'And I bet you can't wait to have her here.'

'The place isn't the same without her,' he admitted. Then, clearly uncomfortable at revealing his dependence, once again he rubbed his hands briskly together. 'Have you managed to get fixed up anywhere else yet?'

Elodie shook her head. 'Not yet, but I do have a bit of good news. In fact, I need a favour, Bill. My dragons are going to be exhibited at a gallery in London.'

'What?' The landlord's surprise was immediately followed by a grin which threatened to split his face in half. 'Didn't I always say you had the gift? Well, I'm blessed. An exhibition in London, eh? You wait till I tell Iris. She'll be over the moon.'

Touched by his genuine delight at her good fortune, Elodie's own pleasure blossomed. 'Yes, well, the point is, I was wondering if I could borrow the pair I made for you and Iris? It would only be for a week or two. They'll be taken great care of, and you'll get them back as soon as the exhibition is over.'

'Of course you can, girl. Just so long as you make it clear they aren't for sale. Not at any price. Well——' he shook his head '—fancy that. Looks as if you're on your way to fame and fortune.'

'You can keep the fame,' Elodie replied, 'but I must admit a little bit of the fortune would be very useful right now.' She sighed, then grinned in an effort to mask her very real fear for her immediate future. It wasn't fair to burden Bill with her problems. He had had enough worry lately. Iris's emergency operation had left him coping single-handed with a pub whose popularity and reputation had been built on both of them working seven days a week.

He turned at the door. 'I knew there was something else. Your yuppie lawyer phoned a few minutes ago. He wants you to call him back. Says it's urgent.' Bill rolled his eyes. 'It always is when they're calling you. But when you want *them* to do anything they take bleddy months over it.' Grunting and sighing, he stumped out of the kitchen.

Taking off her apron, Elodie hunted in her purse for some change then went out to the pay-phone in the passage. Doubtless Steven wanted to know why she had gone off in Neil Munroe's car the other night.

Bracing herself for recriminations, and determined that she was not going to be put up with being browbeaten, Elodie was startled when Steven opened the conversation by suggesting that she think seriously about accepting Neil Munroe's offer.

'B-but I thought—I mean—you said I ought to hold out for a higher price. And what about the right of way?'

'No deal. They won't sell it back. They are absolutely adamant on that point,' Steven replied. 'I don't think you have any choice. In real terms it's only the land Munroe is buying. The cottage itself isn't worth anything. It's inconvenient, uninsurable, and really only fit for demolition.'

'Just a moment, Steven——' Elodie tried to break in.

'I know it's your home.' He raised his voice, drowning her objections. 'But sentiment carries no weight in business. Given that Neil Munroe owns all the land surrounding yours, and considering the present state of the economy, I think it most unlikely he will increase his offer. In fact there is a strong possibility that if you don't accept soon he might even reduce it. After all, in view of the right of way, it's unlikely anyone else will want to buy.'

'That's fine by me,' Elodie retorted. 'I don't want to sell.'

'For God's sake!'

Elodie jerked the phone from her ear as Steven's voice exploded down the line. 'Will you dig your head out of the sand and *listen*? Time is running out. Apart from anything else I can't keep the tax people at bay much longer. I'll have a contract ready by Friday. I shall expect you here in this office before midday to sign it.'

'I can't, Steven, not Friday——' she began, then flinched as his receiver went down with a bang, giving her no chance to explain about the exhibition.

She could hardly believe what had just happened. She was used to Steven being pompous and mildly overbearing. But this had been different. There had been a violence in his voice and manner she didn't understand but found deeply disturbing.

Feeling decidedly shaky, she hung up the phone, taking several deep breaths to calm her jittery nerves before she returned to the kitchen. As she collected her things it suddenly struck her that though she had invited Neil for a meal she hadn't the faintest idea what they were going to eat.

Considering various alternatives helped her overcome the unpleasant after-effects of her phone call to Steven. But there was no escaping the pressure.

The cottage was tidy. The savoury aroma of beef casserole and jacket potatoes wafted from the oven. Wearing a clean pair of jeans and a white lambswool and angora sweater, Elodie gave her hair a thorough brushing then tied it back in a pony-tail with a jade and navy silk scarf. She had no idea

when Neil would arrive. Neither of them had
specified a time. Everything was ready. All she
could do was wait.

That was the hardest part. She couldn't settle.
Leaving the door open so that he would know she
hadn't gone far, Elodie did what she always did
when she needed time to think and space to breathe.
She walked down to the beach.

There was still a faint hint of wood-smoke on the
air. The constant drone and rumble of machinery
and engines from over the hill had ceased. But,
though Elodie welcomed the silence, it was different. The sense of timelessness which had made
the valley so special had been shattered. It would
never be the same again.

Standing at the water's edge, she tossed pebbles
into the gentle swell. The sun was low over the hill
behind her. Its slanting rays turned the billowing
banks of cloud flame and gold in dazzling contrast
to the wine-dark sea. There would be no 'red sky
at night, shepherd's delight' this evening. The ap-
proaching sunset was a fiery display of orange and
purple, heralding more stormy weather.

Pushing her hands into her pockets, Elodie gazed
at the breaking waves. This time last week Neil
Munroe had been simply a hated name. Then, in
the space of a day or two...

She recalled that heart-stopping moment when,
recovering from the shock of his rescue and her
agonising spasm of cramp, she had looked at him
properly for the first time. Vague impressions had
coalesced into the vivid reality of black hair,
bronzed skin, a tall, powerful physique, and glittering blue eyes that cut like lasers through every
defence she raised against them. She could even

hear his voice; deep, quiet, authoritative. Saved from Steven-like pompousness by an underlying note of amusement and self-mockery.

What a strange irony that he should save her life only to change it beyond recognition. She had never talked to anyone the way she had talked to him. Just the way he said her name made her feel special. She could hear it in her head. It was so clear, almost as if . . .

'Elodie?'

She swung round. He was crossing the sand towards her, his suit jacket hooked on one finger and slung over his shoulder.

Remaining where she was, Elodie watched him approach, drinking him in: his lithe stride, his wind-ruffled hair, the gleam of his white teeth as he smiled a greeting.

'I guessed you'd be down here,' he said, bending to kiss her cheek lightly. Then he leaned back, studying her more closely. 'I take it you haven't had the easiest of days?'

She looked away, moving her shoulders. 'You could say that.'

'Anything I can do?'

She raised her head to meet his gaze, overwhelmed by an anguish she did not even attempt to hide. 'Yes. Go away. Leave me in peace.'

His features hardened but his gaze remained compassionate. 'You know I can't do that.'

She nodded wearily.

Neil put his arm around her shoulders and in silence they walked slowly back across the beach. The warm weight of his arm was comforting and as she leaned her head against his shoulder he kissed the top of her head. Elodie didn't know whether

to laugh or cry. This man was her enemy and she
loved him.

'Is there much wildlife in the valley?' he asked
as they started up the path.

Elodie nodded again. 'Foxes, badgers and
rabbits. We used to see them often although they
are generally very shy. But I think the word got
around that Gran was a soft touch. There are
squirrels nesting in the thatch, and during the winter
she used to go out and dig up worms and grubs for
a hedgehog that hadn't hibernated.'

Neil raised his eyebrows. 'Your grandmother was
a very unusual lady.'

'You don't know the half of it,' Elodie said drily.
'One evening she took a biscuit up to bed with her.
This became a regular ritual. No matter how late
we ate supper she must have this biscuit. I didn't
find out for ages that she was having a nightly visit
from a mouse, and the biscuit was for him, not for
her.' She paused, gazing around, swamped by
memories. 'The valley is cool and shady now, but
for real beauty you have to see it in spring. First
come snowdrops and crocuses, then primroses,
daffodils and violets. And by late April there's a
wall-to-wall carpet of bluebells. We have several
species of rhododendron too, but they haven't done
so well over the last couple of years.'

'I'm not surprised.'

Elodie looked quickly up at him. 'Oh? Why not?'

Standing behind her, Neil let his jacket fall to the
ground. He grasped her shoulders. 'Look, Elodie.
Really *look*. Shall I tell you what I see? Half of the
trees are diseased. Those that have fallen or been
blown down are leaning against others or rotting
where they lie. Brambles and tangled undergrowth

are stunting young saplings.' He spun her round to face him. 'This could be a spectacularly beautiful place. But it needs an enormous amount of work.'

'You don't understand,' she cried, whirling round to face him. 'It's meant to be wild. That is its natural beauty.'

'Elodie,' he was impatient, 'it's choking to death.' She tried to break away, but he held her fast. 'Listen, I realise that honouring your grandmother's wishes is terribly important to you. But sweetheart, though I admire your loyalty, I have to tell you that in this instance it's misplaced.'

'You *would* say that,' she flared. 'As my loyalty is standing in the way of your getting what you want it's bound to be misplaced, isn't it? And don't call me sweetheart.'

'Look at me,' he demanded.

She shook her head.

His grip tightened, his fingers biting into her shoulders. She could tell from his quickened breathing that she had made him terribly angry. Well, that was too bad. *She* was angry, and hurt, and confused, and frightened.

'Look at me,' he grated and, before she could refuse, he grasped her chin, forcing her head up. 'Clinging to memories and living in the past won't bring her back, Elodie. Nor will it solve the financial problems you must face. And why shouldn't I call you sweetheart?'

'Because it's too confusing,' Elodie retorted, blinking furiously to disperse tears which, despite her valiant efforts, continued to well up until they spilled over. 'I can't——' Catching her lower lip between her teeth, she shrugged helplessly.

Folding his arms around her, Neil cupped her head and pressed it against his shoulder. 'Don't fight me, darling. There's no need. I want what's best for you.'

'No, you want what's best for *you*,' Elodie mumbled against his shirt front, feeling his body heat and the roughness of his chest hair through the thin material.

'Why shouldn't that be the same thing?' he enquired softly, his lips brushing her forehead.

'Because—because——' Elodie swallowed. 'Because although you call me loving names I haven't the faintest idea what you really feel for me.'

She felt his mouth curve in a brief smile. 'Elodie,' he reproved, 'how can you say such a thing? You know perfectly well what you do to me. Even just standing here like this——' His arms tightened fractionally and he broke off. Their bodies' response to one another made further explanations unnecessary.

'I don't mean...that,' Elodie murmured. 'I mean——'

'I know what you mean,' he said, as she struggled to find the words. 'But it cuts both ways. You haven't told me either.' Cupping her face between his hands, he looked into her tear-washed eyes. 'Tell me, Elodie,' he urged softly. 'Tell me what you *really* feel.'

'I—I——' she whispered breathlessly. 'I—*can't*. Everyone I ever loved has left me. You will too.' She gazed hopelessly into his eyes, praying for his denial, knowing she would not believe it.

His face changed as different expressions passed over it fleetingly like clouds across the sun. Then he held her close once more. And, though being in his arms was the greatest comfort she had ever known, somewhere deep inside she was screaming with terror. For now she knew he would leave because there was something in her that made her unlovable.

'Oh, Elodie.' His voice was a harsh whisper. His arms tightened around her until she could hardly breathe and she realised that he was in the grip of some powerful emotion which had made him forget his own strength.

After a few moments he loosened his hold, but made no move to let her go. 'Sweetheart, parting with people you love is an unavoidable fact of life. It can happen for all kinds of reasons. But fighting shy of feeling because of the risk of loss is totally self-destructive. People who avoid emotional commitment spend their lives searching for something to fill the gap. They chase money, possessions, and power, and wonder why there's no sense of fulfilment. They turn to alcohol, drugs, and sex to try and blot out the loneliness.'

Elodie had a sudden vision of Fenella, and was startled to feel a wave of pity for Neil's glamorous and sophisticated PA.

'I know what I'm talking about,' Neil muttered against her hair, 'and I don't want to see that happen to you.'

Elodie looked up quickly but before she could question him he grinned and she sensed a deliberate change of mood. 'I thought you invited me for a meal. Something certainly smelled delicious when I looked into the kitchen.' With one arm around her shoulders he propelled her up the path towards the cottage. 'I've brought a rather good bottle of wine,' he announced. 'To help us celebrate the good news.'

'What good news?' Elodie demanded, her own mood lifted by his obvious pleasure in what he was about to tell her.

'Giles phoned today. There was an American collector in the gallery when I took the dragons up. He was clearly interested. Anyway, he's been back several times, asking about them. Giles has invited him to the preview on Friday, and he's most anxious to meet you.'

'*Me*?' Elodie gulped. 'What on earth for?'

Shaking his head, Neil laughed. 'Why do you think, idiot? To give you a commission, of course.'

'Oh,' Elodie said. Then, as all the possibilities registered, her eyes widened and she bit her lip, a huge smile of delight spreading across her face. 'Oh.'

'Now that's what I call a jacket potato,' Neil said after his first forkful. 'How do you get the skin so crisp and the inside so fluffy? And I could cut the beef with a spoon, it's so tender. What did you do to it?'

'You can't expect me to give away all my trade secrets,' Elodie chided, thrilled at his admiration of her cooking. 'I'll tell you this, though, and I don't care if you do call me old-fashioned. You won't get the same results with a microwave.'

He burst out laughing. 'Elodie, you're priceless.'

Glowing, she pulled a face at him. 'You make me sound like an antique.'

He leaned towards her across the table. 'You're certainly very rare,' he said softly. The look in his eyes made her heart skip a beat.

They continued their meal. Neil's dry wit reduced Elodie to helpless laughter as he commented on some of the habits and foibles of people he had met through his business dealings. Then he insisted on washing up while she made the coffee.

She carried the tray into the living-room and set it down on the low table in front of the fire. Coming up behind her, he rested his hands lightly on her shoulders.

'This is a very... cosy room,' he murmured, pressing his lips to the side of her neck.

Shuddering with pleasure, Elodie leaned back against his chest. 'The most accurate way to describe it is tiny. Or, if you want to be generous, small. Still,' she sighed, 'it's home.' The word hung in the air between them, like a sword raised to sever the fragile but so welcome truce between them. She wished she hadn't said it. The evening was going so well. They were talking and laughing just like normal couples did. Except that their relationship was not based on mutual attraction, but on a business deal that he wanted and she didn't.

He turned her round. Elodie held her breath. His eyes reflected the dancing flames as they looked deep into hers. 'You make a great beef casserole.'

She felt almost sick with relief and allowed her face to reflect her gratitude as she inclined her head. 'Thank you. But there are other things I do better.'

One dark brow climbed and he smiled his slow barracuda smile, sending tingles of delicious excitement down Elodie's spine as he murmured, 'I can't wait to find out what those are.' His head had inched closer with every word and the last one was spoken with his lips touching hers.

The contact released a great rush of emotion in Élodie. As his arms tightened around her she captured his face in her hands, revelling in the roughness of new beard growth on his jaw as she poured all her love and hope and need into the kiss.

His muffled groan drew a soft answering sound from her own throat and she slid into a whirlpool of sensation.

Something was nagging at the edge of her consciousness. She tried to ignore it but the sound went on and on, a high-pitched bleep, insistent, demanding.

She opened her eyes, and in that same instant Neil tore himself away, cursing under his breath as he grabbed his suit jacket from the back of the armchair, and reached into the inside pocket. Bringing out a small black plastic case the size of a matchbox with rounded edges, he pressed a button on it. The bleeping stopped.

'What is it?' Elodie asked, clutching the back of the settee for support. Her heart was racing and her legs felt weak and shaky.

Neil's face was flushed and beneath his shirt his chest heaved as he struggled to control his ragged breathing. His hair was ruffled and spiky where she had run her fingers through it. 'I'm sorry, sweetheart, I have to go.'

'*What*?' Elodie was stunned.

Snatching up his jacket, Neil quickly put it on, then raked his hands through his hair in an effort to restore it to some sort of order. He came towards her. 'I have to get to a phone,' he explained. 'I left instructions that I was only to be called in certain circumstances.' Bending down, he kissed her cheek. 'I promise you it's a matter of great urgency.'

Elodie nodded and hugged her arms across her midriff, trying hard to hide her bitter disappointment. 'Who did you leave the instructions with?' she asked, more out of a determination to try to make normal conversation than any real curiosity.

But when he glanced round in surprise and said, 'Fenella,' her stomach clenched into a small tight knot.

'Couldn't you come back afterwards?' It was meant simply as a suggestion but to her dismay it emerged sounding like a plea.

He traced the contours of her face with his fingertips. 'I wish I could, sweetheart. But it's likely I shall be working on this until the early hours.'

She wanted to walk up to the road with him, but he wouldn't hear of it, insisting she stay in the cottage by the fire. His goodnight kiss went a long way towards softening the blow of his hasty departure. And later, lying curled up in bed, Elodie tried to find comfort in his final words. 'Sleep well, sweetheart. I'll be in touch.' But her head was full of images of Fenella. Fenella, who worked with Neil and wanted him and warned off anyone who presented even the vaguest threat.

Fenella had called and he had gone. He'd said it was urgent, to do with work. If she loved him she had to believe him, trust him. After all, why would he lie?

CHAPTER TEN

FOR the next few days Elodie worked feverishly to complete the remaining dragons, ready for the exhibition. Never before had she driven herself so hard. When she wasn't doing her shifts at the pub she was in her work-room.

She ate when she remembered, and slept when she was too tired to see properly. Heavy showers and a gusty wind with the chill of autumn in it put paid to any ideas of swimming or walks on the beach. But for once Elodie didn't mind.

Though she enjoyed cooking, the chance of a break from it was very appealing. And the prospect of earning enough to support herself doing something that totally absorbed her was a great spur. But she had a far more pressing reason to keep busy.

She had spent all Tuesday on tenterhooks. Each time Bill or one of the barmaids came into the kitchen she looked up, ready to leave whatever she was doing, expecting to be told there was a phone call for her. But there wasn't. Nor did one come on Wednesday.

'I'll be in touch,' he'd said. The last time Neil had spoken those words he had arrived on the doorstep barely twelve hours later. But this time three days had passed without a word. Something must be wrong. Was it his work? Was he ill? *Or was it her*? Had he simply lost interest?

Doubt and insecurity crowded in to gnaw at her fragile self-confidence.

After leaving the pub on Thursday afternoon, she screwed up her courage, went to the call-box in the village, and phoned Neil's office.

Elodie knew she wasn't imagining the malicious pleasure in Fenella's voice as she announced smoothly that Neil was unavailable.

Refusing to be intimidated, though she was gripping the receiver so tightly that her knuckles gleamed white beneath the taut skin, Elodie asked if that meant Neil was in a meeting. 'If he is out of the office can you tell me when you expect him back?'

'I'm afraid I don't have that information,' Fenella drawled. 'Neil has your address. If he wants to contact you, he will. Now you must excuse me, we are very busy at the moment. Goodbye, Miss Swann.'

The line went dead and Elodie was left staring helplessly at the receiver. She had been deliberately and expertly stonewalled. And, though Fenella's tone had been spiteful and gloating, she had not said one word which could honestly be termed offensive.

So Elodie returned home and worked even harder. She concentrated fiercely on the clay, the glaze, the temperature of her ancient kiln, trying desperately not to speculate. There was bound to be a reason for his silence, and when he came back he would explain. *If he came back*.

Of course he would come back. If for no other reason than to fly her to London for the preview. As it was entirely due to him that her work was being exhibited, their non-arrival would reflect as badly on him as on her.

Tomorrow was Friday, *the* day. He was bound to come tomorrow, and the endless, agonising wait would be over.

She clung to this thought as if it were a life raft through an almost sleepless night.

At six o'clock on Friday morning she got up, unable to remain in her rumpled bed a moment longer. After showering and washing her hair, she carefully packed the dragons. The very thought of food made her stomach heave, but she forced down a slice of toast and a cup of coffee, tortured by vivid memories of breakfast with Neil in his flat.

What if he didn't come? He would. Of course he would. She had to believe that, otherwise...

Elodie had no idea how she got through the morning. She must have behaved quite normally for no one made any comment. One of the girls did remark that she looked a bit tired, and she overheard another speculate that Iris's imminent return could be the reason she was quieter than usual. But that was all. Yet inside she felt as though she was falling to pieces.

At two o'clock she said goodbye to the kitchen staff. Holding her breath, praying he would be there and giving herself all sorts of reasons why he might not be, she went out to the car park.

One swift, searching glance was enough. Yet still she hesitated. Then, head down, lips compressed to stop them quivering, she hurried across the road, desperate to reach the sanctuary of the cottage as fast as she could.

Once out of the village, she pulled a tissue from her bag and angrily scrubbed away the tears.

A heavy lorry thundered towards her and she flattened herself against the hedge, closing her eyes against the wake of swirling dust.

No sooner had it passed than she heard the sound of another engine. She waited, head averted, expecting another gust of turbulence. Instead a car stopped alongside her. As she wiped her eyes again, she heard the hum of an electric window then that deep familiar voice.

'I was hoping to get to the pub in time to pick you up, but the traffic out of town was horrendous.'

Not trusting herself to speak, Elodie smiled radiantly. He had come! Hadn't she known all along that he would?

Leaning over, he opened the passenger door for her and she got in.

He didn't return her smile. 'What's the matter with your eyes?' he asked, his brows drawn together in concern. 'Was it the dust?'

Thankful that he had presented her with a ready-made excuse, Elodie nodded quickly and wiped them again. She wanted to hold him and kiss him and hammer him with her fists. Her head was bursting with questions, all clamouring to be answered.

But the big car was already gathering speed. Fastening her seatbelt, she glanced up at him. Chills feathered down her spine at his cold, hard expression. Her smile died and her joy evaporated. Dread sat like a suffocating weight on her chest, restricting her breathing and drying her throat.

When they pulled on to the verge at the top of the lane a few moments later, she had begun to tremble.

Switching off the engine, Neil undid his seatbelt and half turned so that he was facing her. 'Elodie, I'm afraid I've got some bad news for you.' Reaching out, he took her hand, and looked up, his frown deepening. 'Your hand's like ice. Why are you shaking?'

Elodie swallowed hard. 'I—I think I——' Know what you're going to say, she finished silently. She couldn't go on.

'Tell me in a moment. First there's something I must tell you.' His expression was grave, and his direct look was a knife plunging into her heart.

But even at this moment she had to admire him. For there was one thing Neil Munroe had never lacked, and that was the courage to do what he believed in, no matter what the consequences.

'There's no easy way to say this. And I wish I didn't have to.' He paused.

'Please,' Elodie said through gritted teeth, 'let's get it over with. Just tell me.'

He pressed her fingers. 'As a result of something you told me a few days ago I asked my legal department to do some investigating. They have found evidence proving that Steven Lockwood, your solicitor, has been using your trust fund to play the stock market.'

Neil's gaze fell to her hands for a moment. Then he met her eyes once more. 'Elodie, I'm afraid he has lost a great deal of money. Your money.'

Dumbfounded, Elodie could only stare at him. Having prepared herself for something entirely different, she simply couldn't take in what he had said.

And when it did register she couldn't believe it. 'Steven?' she croaked. 'No.' She shook her head. 'No, there must be some mistake.'

Then she remembered the snatch of conversation she had overheard when Steven was on the phone to his broker. But she still didn't want to accept it, for if it was true...

Releasing her hand, Neil leaned forward and picked up the car phone. He dialled and Elodie heard the receptionist at Steven's office answer. Silently Neil handed the phone to her. 'Ask him.'

Shaking like a leaf, her heart pounding as shock sent her nervous system into overdrive, Elodie cleared her throat and asked to speak to Steven.

'About time,' he said by way of greeting, his edgy impatience clearly audible in the confined space of the car. 'Where are you anyway? I expected you to come in and sign the contract this morning. It's important we get this deal sewn up before Munroe——'

'Steven,' Elodie interrupted, gazing blindly through the windscreen, 'have you been using my money to buy shares?'

The silence was not long, a few seconds at most. But it was enough. Elodie sank back against the thickly padded upholstery, shattered.

'No need to ask who told you,' Steven replied bitterly. 'All right, what I did wasn't strictly ethical, but you wanted to keep the property and there was no way you could do that *and* pay the inheritance tax. I took a chance. It was a high-risk investment, but the potential rewards were enormous.'

Elodie's mouth was so dry it was difficult to talk. 'But you lost. You wouldn't let *me* touch the money, but you did, and you lost it.'

'Listen, Elodie.' Steven's tone was urgent. 'You only met Neil Munroe a few days ago and, despite all my warnings, you've obviously fallen for the man's slick professional charm. Perhaps you've forgotten the grief his letters caused your grandmother, and you, in the months before she died.'

Elodie winced. Beside her, listening to every word, Neil sat motionless, his expression glacial.

'He wants your property, Elodie,' Steven went on, 'and he'll do his damnedest to discredit anyone who tries to block him. I'm not a high-flyer and I don't have his charisma, but everything I've done was with the best of intentions.' His tone had changed to one of angry affront. 'I've risked everything for you, Elodie, and I have to say your attitude is most hurtful.' He hung up.

Mouth curling in disgust, Neil took the receiver from Elodie's hand and slammed it down. 'I'll give him credit for one thing—he can certainly think on his feet.'

Resting her elbow on the arm-rest, Elodie stared into space, chewing her thumbnail. She didn't know what to say or even think.

She felt Neil's eyes on her and sensed his growing fury and frustration but was powerless to do anything to ease them. She hadn't seen or heard from him since Monday, and as yet he had offered no reason or excuse. Who did she believe? What was the truth?

'God almighty!' The words burst from Neil with barely suppressed violence. Getting out, he slammed the door and came round to her side. 'Come on.' He opened the passenger door. 'We don't have time to discuss this now. I'll bring the dragons up to the car while you get ready.'

He locked the door behind her and as they started down the path the air between them was so charged, it made Elodie's skin prickle.

As they entered the cottage, Elodie dumped her bag on the kitchen table and grasped the back of the wooden chair, her head bent. 'I can't face it,' she said, her voice low.

Neil had taken the kettle to the sink to fill. 'What are you talking about?' he demanded over his shoulder.

'Tonight.' She looked up at him, feeling utterly wretched. 'The party, the Press, all those people. Not after this.' She shook her head. And it wasn't over yet. There was more to come. She knew that as surely as she knew her own name.

Plugging the kettle in, Neil switched it on, then leaned back against the work-top, folding his arms and crossing one foot over the other.

'Now you listen to me.' His features were as hard and cold as wind-swept granite. 'There are things you have to know about, but now is not the time. Not only is this exhibition the key to your entire future, a lot of people have gone to a lot of trouble on your behalf. I can understand your being nervous. I'll even allow for a certain amount of artistic temperament. But pure bad manners? That is something I will not tolerate. You are going, Elodie, if I have to drag you there.'

Stiff with rage, her chin tilted, Elodie opened her mouth.

'Not another word,' he warned softly, his eyes glittering slits in a mask of contempt. Realising he was in deadly earnest, Elodie flushed scarlet, bit her lip, and ran upstairs.

Half an hour later she had showered and changed into a flowing skirt of moss-green silk jersey teamed with a bronze-gold full-sleeved silk shirt. Brushed and left loose, her hair lay in gleaming waves over her shoulders. In an effort to disguise the strain of the past few days she had highlighted her eyes with bronze shadow and darkened the tips of her long lashes with mascara. A touch of blusher added some much-needed colour to her cheeks, and coral lip-gloss gave her mouth a ripe lustre.

Neil entered the kitchen as she came breathlessly down the stairs. 'All the boxes are in the car,' he announced, his back to her as he closed the door. 'I've made some tea and the fire is——' Turning as he spoke, he broke off, visibly startled.

Elodie's heart sank. 'Isn't this suitable?' She smoothed down her skirt. 'I didn't know what——'

His gaze swept over her with such thoroughness that she felt as though she had been stroked. Then he smiled. 'It's perfect. You look—you are,' he corrected himself, 'very beautiful.'

Elodie was stunned. In spite of her doubts and confusion, delight exploded inside her like a sun-burst. 'Thank you,' she murmured shyly, and busied herself transferring her purse, comb, and some tissues to her bronze-gold evening bag while he poured the tea.

'Drink this; it will keep body and soul together until the buffet.' He passed her a mug. 'There's just one thing...'

Her head flew up. 'Yes?'

'Don't panic,' he soothed. 'I was simply won-dering about the path. The rain has left it pretty muddy in places. A long skirt and heeled shoes——'

'No problem,' Elodie cut in, gulping down the last of her tea. 'This material doesn't crease, so I can hitch it up, wear wellies to the car, and carry my shoes.'

'Well, that's a relief,' he announced. 'At least I'm spared having to lay down my coat for you to walk on.' He drained his own mug.

Deeply relieved at the lightening of the atmosphere between them, even though she knew there were still many questions unanswered, Elodie tilted her head to one side.

'I can just imagine what they'd say at the preview if you turned up soaking wet, plastered with mud, and offered that as an excuse.'

'They'd question my sanity,' he conceded. 'Come on, we'd better get moving. What about a coat? I know you're not cold now, but by tonight you'll need something a lot warmer than that.' He indicated her fine wool wrap, patterned in moss-green, gold, and black.

Elated at his concern, Elodie dashed upstairs again. She returned a few moments later carrying a single-breasted camel jacket with a huge shawl collar.

'Ready?' Neil moved to the door.

'One last thing.' Elodie scooped up her bag and shoes and peered into the living-room. She glanced round at Neil, a tiny frown of concern puckering her forehead. 'Don't think I'm not grateful, but that's quite a fire.'

'Don't worry,' he reassured her, 'I've banked it well down. And with the guard in front it's perfectly safe.' He came to her side and rested his hand on her shoulder. Elodie found the warm weight of it very comforting.

'It could be nearly midnight before we get back,' he said. 'You'll be exhausted. And according to the forecast there's more rain on the way. For a welcome home there's nothing to beat a glowing fire.'

She nodded, and smiled up at him. 'I guess my nerves are showing.'

'You're nervous? Whatever for?' His gleaming eyes held hers and she felt as if she was drowning. 'Elodie Swann, with your beauty, brains, and talent you'll have them eating out of your hand.'

The evening was a roaring success. To Elodie's amazement and delight, her dragons caught the attention of the Press. 'Fresh young talent,' was just one of the phrases she heard repeated as Giles piloted her through the crowd, and instructed Neil to make sure she circulated.

She was interviewed and photographed. She met the American collector, a tall, thin Texan with a crew-cut and gold-rimmed glasses. His blunt enthusiasm lifted her spirits even higher. As soon as he had obtained her promise to make him a pair of dragons, offering her a sum she hardly dared believe, he excused himself and hurried down to the taxi that was waiting to rush him to the airport.

'You are handling this like a veteran,' Neil murmured in her ear after rescuing her from a loud-voiced woman, wearing a vast purple dress and orange hair, who was determined to explain to Elodie the sexual significance of dragons in medieval legend.

'I had no *idea*,' she whispered back, wide-eyed.

At first she had been overawed. But as Neil supplemented the programme notes on each exhibitor with snippets of slanderous gossip she quickly relaxed, unable to suppress her giggles.

While leaving her to cope on her own as much as possible, he would appear at her side the moment she needed some moral support, or protection from guests whose interest and enthusiasm, aided by free champagne, went over the top.

As the evening progressed, and her smile grew more spontaneous as she talked to different people, all sorts of changes were going on inside her head. She was seeing things so differently. It was like looking at the view from a mountain-top after living in a narrow canyon.

Of course, there were still many questions to be answered and much to be discussed. But her fears that Neil was interested in her only for her property were dissolving. There was only one dark cloud on an otherwise clear horizon: Fenella. That was something which had to be faced, and brought out into the open.

Elodie looked beyond the people grouped around her, who were earnestly discussing the merits of the new realism, and caught Neil's eye. His brief but undeniable wink filled her with a bubbling happiness that even the champagne couldn't match. She knew then that she couldn't hold back any longer.

Tonight, when they got home, she would tell him what was in her heart. She would say the words which only days ago were unthinkable. It would take all her courage, especially as it meant she was facing Neil with a choice between herself and Fenella. It was the biggest gamble of her life and there was no guarantee that she would win.

As they flew back to Cornwall, Elodie huddled into her coat. 'You were right about my needing this.' She smiled at him. 'You've been right about a lot of things; I see that now.'

In the light from the instrument panel she saw a
dry grin flicker across his mouth. 'I'm glad to hear
it.'

Her pleasure tonight had been doubled by having
him share it. Being solitary might be safer, but it
was a barren, joyless existence. There were risks but
she was prepared to take them. She was ready to
let go of the past. *But was he*?

As he helped her out of the helicopter she reached
up impulsively and kissed him on the mouth.

'Mmm.' He slid his arm around her waist and
smiled down at her. 'That was nice. Was it for any
particular reason?'

'Yes,' Elodie nodded. 'For lots of reasons, actually. I'll tell you about them.' She held him at
arm's length as he tried to draw her closer. 'When
we get home,' she insisted, laughing even though
her heart was beginning to pound in nervous
anticipation.

'Then stop wasting time, woman, and get in the
car.' His gleaming gaze sent her pulse-rate soaring.
'There are going to be changes, Elodie. I'm not
prepared to wait any longer.'

He wouldn't explain, and she was still pondering
his cryptic statement as they turned into the road
leading to the lane.

She was so absorbed in her thoughts that she had
been gazing for several seconds at the flickering
orange glow over the valley before it registered on
her conscious mind.

'Your men aren't still working at this time of
night, surely?' Glancing at Neil, she grinned. 'I
dread to think what they'll be claiming in overtime.'

'Of course not.' He sounded puzzled. 'There's some by-law or other which prohibits the burning of——'

But Elodie wasn't listening. As they rounded the bend she could see that the source of the ominous flickering glow was *in* the valley, not beyond it. 'No,' she whispered. 'Oh, please, no.'

She was already kicking off her shoes and reaching behind the seat for the carrier containing her wellies as Neil braked to an abrupt stop on the verge above the lane.

'Elodie, wait,' he called urgently as she flung open the door, stuffed her feet into her boots, and started running.

Branches snagged her clothes and hair. She slipped and fell on the muddy path. Scrambling up, heedless of her scratched hands and dirt-streaked skirt, she raced on down the path, her horrified gaze fixed on the leaping flames.

'No!' she screamed, skidding to a panting halt at the edge of the scorched lawn. Most of the thatch and roof timbers had already fallen in. The window glass had gone, and flames were consuming the wooden frames and lintels. Heat and smoke seared her throat, making her cough. Her eyes streamed as she dashed the tears away with a muddy hand.

She wasn't aware of Neil until he put his arm around her shoulders. 'Come away, Elodie,' he urged. 'There's nothing you can do.'

She flinched away from him. After the glorious success of the preview, this devastating aftermath struck like a dagger at her heart. She had tried to imagine what it would be like, leaving the cottage. In all the different scenes she had played over in her head—how she would leave, when she would

leave, where she would go—the cottage had remained just as she had always known it. Timeless,
part of the valley, exactly as it had been for the last
hundred years. Was this Fenella's revenge? No.
Elodie remembered how Fenella had backed down
in the face of Neil's wrath. No matter how bitter
her anger, she wouldn't have dared go this far. Then
who? How?

'Don't touch me,' she whispered through paper-
dry lips.

Neil's face betrayed a moment's total shock.
'Elodie? Surely you don't think *I* had anything to
do with this?'

She looked up. Through her tears he was a
blurred, shimmering figure, somehow remote. She
had never felt so alone. Her throat was stiff with
grief and her voice cracked. 'No, I don't believe
you did. But don't pretend you're sorry. After all,
think of the time and money you've been saved.'

Despite the fierce heat she was chilled to the
marrow of her bones. She had thought she was
ready to move on. But nothing had prepared her
for the total destruction of her home and all her
possessions. Her entire past was being consumed
by the flames. There was nothing left to remind her
of who she was or where she had come from.

'Please——' she made a vague warding-off
gesture '—leave me alone.'

Neil's features were a gilded mask. But though
his eyes reflected the dancing flames they were as
cold as arctic ice. 'You can't stay here,' he said
flatly.

'I can do what I like,' Elodie cried. 'I'll sign the contract tomorrow. With no home I have no choice. But right now this is still my property, and I want you to go.'

'I can see what Eddie Merrin says,' Reith had
exulted, running a hand across a brow no longer
placid. 'Now get on and put the two, lady, and I want
some more . . .'

CHAPTER ELEVEN

NEIL gave no sign of having heard. Grasping her
arm, he thrust her ahead of him up the path, ignoring her struggles.

'Let go of me,' Elodie gritted, crying out as his
fingers bit mercilessly into her flesh.

Neil remained silent but harsh breathing and lips
compressed to a mere slash in the stony mask of
his face indicated control stretched to snapping-
point.

Bundling her into the car, he slammed the door
shut. Once in his seat he picked up the car phone
and called the fire brigade. Then, engine roaring
and tyres screaming, he spun the car round and set
it racing back towards the village.

By the time they reached the pub, Elodie felt
strangely calm. She had retreated deep inside
herself. There was no pain. It was peaceful, this
numbness. She was shaking and cold, but it didn't
matter. Nothing mattered any more.

She had been aware of Neil glancing frequently
in her direction as he drove. She had watched him
pick up the car phone and call someone. Or maybe
it had been more than one person. It wasn't important. She had heard his voice, but the words
had had no meaning. Everything was happening at
a distance, as if she were looking down the wrong
end of a telescope.

Bill, in pyjamas and dressing-gown, was on the
doorstep to meet them. He exchanged a few brief

words with Neil then disappeared, and Neil half led, half carried her upstairs and into a bedroom.

As Neil was removing her coat, Bill arrived with a mug which had something warm and milky in it.

She couldn't stop shaking and Neil had to hold the mug so that she could drink. She didn't want to bother but he insisted and she didn't have the strength to argue.

Then another man came in. He had a small black case, which he opened on the dressing-table. When he turned round the light glinted on something in his hand. She felt a stinging sensation in her arm and everything went mercifully dark.

Elodie opened her eyes slowly. Light was streaming in through the curtains. She blinked, trying to focus her mind as she gazed at the flower-strewn material which moved gently in the breeze from the open window. They weren't her curtains. This wasn't her bedroom.

Where was she? Her head felt muzzy, as though it were stuffed with cotton wool. Gradually all that had happened started coming back to her. Steven's theft of her money, the fire that had destroyed her home. The memories were blunted by this strange hazy detachment.

She heard the door open. Turning, she looked up into the concerned face of Neil Munroe.

Freshly shaved, wearing jeans and a Norwegian-style sweater over a lemon polo shirt, his hair still damp, he looked more handsome than she had ever seen him. She closed her eyes.

'How are you feeling?'

Elodie's breath caught on a sob. He actually sounded as though he cared. Her eyes filled. 'Please go away.'

'Elodie, listen——'

'You have nothing to say that I want to hear. Please, just go.'

'I know what caused the fire——'

'Great, terrific.' A spark of her old spirit cut through the wretchedness that clouded her brain. 'That makes all the difference.'

Neil's features hardened. 'Right, that's it,' he snapped. Straightening up, he headed for the door. 'Get up. I'm taking you back to the cottage.'

'You're not taking me anywhere,' she retorted.

'You have five minutes to get dressed.'

She sat up, pushing her tumbled hair back. 'Don't you ever listen? I said——'

Neil grasped the door-handle. 'Five minutes, Elodie. And if you are not down by then I'll dress you myself. I took your clothes off. I won't have any trouble putting them back on.' Opening the door, he strode out, leaving her staring, shocked and speechless, after him.

After washing her face and hands at the corner sink, Elodie dressed quickly. Whatever else Neil Munroe might be, he was a man of his word. Let him come back in five minutes. He wasn't going to find her cowering in bed.

As she tucked her silk blouse into the waistband of her mud-streaked skirt there was a brief, brisk knock on the door. Elodie didn't have a chance to reply before it opened and he strode in.

'Good,' he said curtly. 'You've saved me a job. Downstairs. Now,' he rapped.

Elodie bristled. 'Don't you use that tone with me.'

Neil's eyes glittered and his voice was dangerously soft. 'You accuse me of making capital out of the destruction of your home and you *dare* question my tone of voice?'

Elodie's throat was suddenly dry and a shiver of real fear slid like ice-water down her spine.

'Get down those stairs,' he hissed and, grabbing her coat, she obeyed.

As they reached the bottom, Bill hurried along the passage to meet them.

'All right, my bird?' His smile was a mixture of reassurance and concern. 'It's all over the village about the fire. Thank God you weren't home when it started, that's all I can say. The firemen said that lintel was as good as a time-bomb.'

Elodie stared at him, then rubbed her forehead with her fingertips, trying to clear her head. 'I'm sorry, Bill. I don't understand. What are you talking about?'

'The fire. Whoever built the cottage used an old ship's mast as a lintel. Over the years they dry right out, and, being soaked in tar, they're a terrible fire hazard.'

Bill shook his head. 'It only needs a bit of burning soot to fall on it. You can't tell it's happening, see? It smoulders away out of sight then suddenly it'll catch.' He cocked a sympathetic eyebrow at her. 'The firemen said your chimney didn't look like it had been swept this year.'

Elodie swallowed. Her throat felt tight. 'No,' she murmured. She had intended having it done in the spring, but her grandmother's death had pushed it right out of her mind. If anyone was to blame for the fire it was her.

She looked up at Neil. His face was totally expressionless but his eyes, as they met hers, were more searing than the flames which had consumed the cottage.

Grasping her arm, he hustled her towards the back door. 'Will you excuse us, Bill?' He tossed the words over his shoulder.

The landlord raised a hand. 'That's all right. I expect you got things to do. Elodie, there's a bed for you here for as long as you want it. At least that's one thing you needn't go worrying about.'

'Th—thanks, Bill,' she called after him as he disappeared down the passage. Next moment she was out on the car park and, seconds later, strapped in beside Neil as the big car hurtled out of the village.

She moistened her lips. 'Why are you taking me back to the cottage?'

'To say goodbye.'

Her quick indrawn breath hissed softly as his answer, delivered in a flat tone that matched his expression, cut her to the quick. Yet what else could she have expected?

The fire engines had scored deep ruts in the grass verge at the top of the lane.

'You go on down,' Neil ordered, braking to a stop. She glanced uncertainly at him and his voice softened slightly as he added, 'You'll want a moment alone.'

As she stood on the edge of the scorched lawn, her hands in her coat pockets, Elodie realised that he understood her better than she did herself. She gazed at the blackened ruins of what had been her home. The acrid smell of wet soot and charred wood caught in her nostrils. Last night it had all seemed like a terrible nightmare. This morning she accepted the stark reality. With a deep, shuddering sigh she turned away and followed the path down to the beach.

Standing just out of reach of the crashing surf, the wind blowing her hair off her face, she licked her lips and tasted the salt. She would not come here again. The fire had closed a door on her past. She had nothing but the clothes she was wearing and the contents of her evening bag. It was strange. She didn't feel anything.

A single scalding tear welled up, hovered for a moment on her lashes, then spilled over to trickle down her cheek. *Neil.* Another tear fell, and another. Closing her eyes, Elodie lifted her face to the grey sky as sobs shook her.

'I thought I'd find you here.'

She whirled round. Quickly wiping her wet cheeks with her palms, she took a deep breath. 'I just wanted——' She bit her lip, swallowing hard. 'My grandmother once told me that "if only" and "too late" are the saddest words in any language. How can I ever apologise? I said some terrible things——'

He covered her mouth with his fingers. 'Hush. Forget it. You were in deep shock.'

Drawing herself up, she met his gaze. 'If this is to be goodbye——' Her chin quivered, and she swallowed hard, fiercely blinking away tears. 'You have been kinder than I deserve. If you could give me a lift into town I'm ready to sign that contract now.'

Neil rested his hands on her shoulders. 'What do you mean, *goodbye*? I'm not going anywhere and nor, if I have anything to do with it, are you.'

Elodie stared at him, hardly daring to breathe. 'But you said—wasn't that why you brought me here?'

'I brought you here to say goodbye to your old life, Elodie. I said there were going to be changes, that I wasn't prepared to wait any longer.'

She nodded quickly. 'Yes, but I thought you were talking about the sale.'

He studied her face, and once again she was totally unable to divine what he was thinking. 'I'm afraid the deal is off.'

Elodie actually felt the blood drain from her face. 'What do you mean? You wanted this land. You said it was vital to your whole scheme. Besides...' She hesitated, then, driven by the desperation of her situation, plunged on, 'I *must* sell. I have nothing left.'

Eyes gleaming, Neil smiled down at her. 'On the contrary, you are a wealthy woman.'

Dumbstruck, Elodie stared at him. 'P-please,' she stammered at last, 'don't make jokes. I can't——'

He sobered at once. 'Sweetheart, I might occasionally be a thoughtless bastard, but I'm not a sadist. What I said is the truth. I was going to tell you last night after we got home from the preview. Don't you remember? I said——'

There are things you have to know about, but now is not the time. She recalled his words.

'Yes, but——'

'Elodie, once I had found out about Steven Lockwood embezzling your trust fund, I didn't just leave it there. With the partners' co-operation we ran a thorough check to see if he had been dipping

into other funds. During this check we struck gold
in the form of a copy of your father's will.'

Elodie looked bewildered. 'I don't understand.'

'The copy we found cancelled the trust fund ar-
rangement. It was signed, dated, and properly witnessed. This was the will which should have been
administered. Lockwood thought he had destroyed
it. He didn't realise there was a copy. Fortunately
it had been misfiled.'

'But—what does it mean?' Elodie was finding it
hard to take in.

'It means, my love, that Lockwood is facing cri-
minal charges, and within a few days you will have
access to the money which was yours all along. It's
less than it should be, but there is still a fair sum.'

'My love', he had called her 'my love'. Elodie's
grip on his forearms tightened. She felt distinctly
light-headed.

'Why won't you buy my land?' she pleaded. 'You
said the beach and my side of the valley were really
important to the development.' Her mouth curved
in an uncertain smile. 'Do you know what's really
ironic? Losing the cottage severed all my ties with
the past. You were right. You've been right about
so many things. A place means nothing without
someone you care for very deeply to share it with.'

Apart from a slight lift of the eyebrows, his face
remained expressionless. 'You must miss your
grandmother very much.'

Elodie moistened her lips. 'Yes, I do. But that
wasn't what I meant.' She could feel her face
growing hot. It was now or never. There had been
too many doubts, too many misunderstandings. She
had to tell him and take the consequences.

'What I'm trying to say——' She swallowed. Still he waited, calm, unmoving, looking as though he had all the time in the world. Yet she had seen for herself how busy he was, how much he had to think about in a day. Her courage wavered. 'Perhaps——'

With a muffled growl, Neil clasped her face between his hands. 'For God's sake, Elodie. Say it.'

'I love you,' she blurted, then clapped her hands over her mouth, her eyes huge with shock at her own recklessness.

Neil tipped his head back and laughed. 'At last!' he cried. 'Woman, you don't know what you've put me through. The day I hauled you out on to this beach I vowed you would be mine. I didn't realise I was facing the biggest challenge of my entire life.' He folded her in his arms, and rested his cheek on the top of her head. 'But I wouldn't have missed a single moment.'

As Elodie slid her own arms around him happiness flowed like heady wine along her veins. 'Really?' She could still hardly believe what was happening. An hour ago her whole world had lain in fragments. Now she had more than she had ever dreamed of.

'Really,' he reassured her, then held her away from him, smiling down into her upturned face. 'Didn't I tell you I always get what I want in the end?'

'Neil,' she began hesitantly, 'about Fenella ...'

To her unutterable relief the only change in his expression was a lift of his eyebrows in mild surprise.

'What about her?'

Elodie screwed up her courage. 'Look, I'm not sophisticated, and maybe it's selfish and possessive of me but——'

'Never mind the preamble, just say what's bothering you.' The gentleness in his voice helped her over the final hurdle.

She swallowed. 'I won't share you. It's her or me. You have to choose.'

The corners of his mouth twitched. 'There is no choice, Elodie,' he said gravely.

Her heart felt as though a giant hand was squeezing it as she searched his face. What did he mean?

Then he smiled. 'There never was. What happened between Fenella and me was over a long time ago. And once I met you——' he shook his head as if surprised at his own feelings '—other women ceased to exist.'

Relief broke over Elodie like a warm wave, leaving her weak and trembling and ridiculously close to tears. But now they were tears of joy.

'I have everything I want.' He gave a satisfied sigh.

Bewildered, Elodie looked up at him. 'That's not true. It was my land that brought you here in the first place. Yet now you say you don't want it.'

'Ah, your land.' He nodded. 'How do you feel about its being cleared and landscaped as part of the project, but remaining in your name? And I'll build us a luxury bungalow, with a studio, on the cottage site.'

Radiant, Elodie gazed up at him. 'Oh,' she breathed. 'Oh.'

'Do I take that as an acceptance of my proposal?'

'M-marriage?' she gulped.

He nodded again. 'I won't settle for anything less. It's taken me this long to find you. I'm not prepared to risk losing you.'

Her eyes shimmered as they held his. 'Oh, Neil. You couldn't lose me if you tried. I'm yours, now and always.'

His smile faded. 'I'll make you happy, Elodie. And I give you my solemn oath, you will be loved for as long as I live.'

Her eyes filled, and, unable to speak, she flung her arms around his neck, and rained kisses on his face. Neil's hold on her tightened, and he sought her mouth.

When, long moments later, he reluctantly let her go, Elodie knew that, for her, life was just about to begin.

Turning her so that her back was against his chest, he folded his arms across the front of her shoulders. 'This is where it all started,' he murmured, his breath warm against her ear as they gazed out across the grey lumpy sea. 'I watched you, you know. You were like a mermaid, so lithe and golden.' He paused. 'I've got a confession to make.'

Utterly secure, knowing that she had found her real home at last in the arms of this man, Elodie smiled up at him. 'Go on, then. Confess.'

'I wished that cramp on you.'

'You *what*?' Elodie laughed.

He nodded. 'I had already decided I was going to rescue you, whether you needed it or not. Then I saw you really were in trouble.'

'So that's how you managed to reach me so quickly.'

His arms tightened. 'You were so damned beautiful. You don't know what it cost me to keep my hands off you.'

Kissing his jaw, Elodie murmured, 'It wasn't all one-sided. You made me feel . . .' Suddenly shy, she bent her head.

Turning her to face him, holding her close within the protective circle of his arms, Neil ran his lips lightly down her face until he reached her mouth, which he cherished, nibbled and teased with the tip of his tongue. 'Nice things?' he asked in a soft, husky voice.

'Mmm.' The sound, little more than a sigh, came from deep in Elodie's throat. Already his touch was weaving its wonderful magic. Her blood felt like warm honey in her veins, and the centre of her body throbbed with a growing urgency. 'Wonderful things,' she whispered against his mouth.

Raising his head, he looked into her half-closed eyes, his own gleaming with love, laughter and a hunger that made her tingle. 'I think it's time we went home.'

Elodie smiled up at him. 'Yes, please.'

Next Month's Romances

Each month you can choose from a world of variety in romance with Mills & Boon. Below are the new titles to look out for next month, why not ask either Mills & Boon Reader Service or your Newsagent to reserve you a copy of the titles you want to buy – just tick the titles you would like to order and either post to Reader Service or take it to any Newsagent and ask them to order your books.

Please save me the following titles:	Please tick	√
A HONEYED SEDUCTION	**Diana Hamilton**	
PASSIONATE POSSESSION	**Penny Jordan**	
MOTHER OF THE BRIDE	**Carole Mortimer**	
DARK ILLUSION	**Patricia Wilson**	
FATE OF HAPPINESS	**Emma Richmond**	
THE ALPHA MAN	**Kay Thorpe**	
HUNGARIAN RHAPSODY (This book is free with THE ALPHA MAN)	**Jessica Steele**	
NOTHING LESS THAN LOVE	**Vanessa Grant**	
LOVE'S VENDETTA	**Stephanie Howard**	
CALL UP THE WIND	**Anne McAllister**	
TOUCH OF FIRE	**Joanna Neil**	
TOMORROW'S HARVEST	**Alison York**	
THE STOLEN HEART	**Amanda Browning**	
NO MISTAKING LOVE	**Jessica Hart**	
THE BEGINNING OF THE AFFAIR	**Marjorie Lewty**	
CAUSE FOR LOVE	**Kerry Allyne**	
RAPTURE IN THE SANDS	**Sandra Marton**	

If you would like to order these books from Mills & Boon Reader Service please send £1.70 per title to: Mills & Boon Reader Service, P.O. Box 236, Croydon, Surrey, CR9 3RU and quote your Subscriber No:..(If applicable) and complete the name and address details below. Alternatively, these books are available from many local Newsagents including W.H.Smith, J.Menzies, Martins and other paperback stockists from 11th September 1992.

Name:...

Address:...

....Post Code:........................

To Retailer: If you would like to stock M&B books please contact your regular book/magazine wholesaler for details.

You may be mailed with offers from other reputable companies as a result of this application. If you would rather not take advantage of these opportunities please tick box ☐